"R.J. Patterson ... engaged and interested. I loo... ...ore from this talented author."

- *Aaron Patterson*
bestselling author of SWEET DREAMS

DEAD SHOT

"Small town life in southern Idaho might seem quaint and idyllic to some. But when local newspaper reporter Cal Murphy begins to uncover a series of strange deaths that are linked to a sticky spider web of deception, the lid on the peaceful town is blown wide open. Told with all the energy and bravado of an old pro, first-timer R.J. Patterson hits one out of the park his first time at bat with *Dead Shot*. It's that good."

- *Vincent Zandri*
bestselling author of THE REMAINS

"You can tell R.J. knows what it's like to live in the newspaper world, but with *Dead Shot*, he's proven that he also can write one heck of a murder mystery."

- *Josh Katzowitz*
NFL writer for CBSSports.com
& author of Sid Gillman: Father of the Passing Game

"Patterson has a mean streak about a mile wide and puts his two main characters through quite a horrible ride, which makes for good reading."

- *Richard D.*, *reader*

DEAD LINE

"This book kept me on the edge of my seat the whole time. I didn't really want to put it down. R.J. Patterson has hooked me. I'll be back for more."

- *Bob Behler*
3-time Idaho broadcaster of the year
and play-by-play voice for Boise State football

"Like a John Grisham novel, from the very start I was pulled right into the story and couldn't put the book down. It was as if I personally knew and cared about what happened to each of the main characters. Every chapter ended with so much excitement and suspense I had to continue to read until I learned how it ended, even though it kept me up until 3:00 A.M.
- *Ray F., reader*

DEAD IN THE WATER

"In Dead in the Water, R.J. Patterson accurately captures the action-packed saga of a what could be a real-life college football scandal. The sordid details will leave readers flipping through the pages as fast as a hurry-up offense."
- Mark Schlabach,
ESPN college sports columnist and
co-author of *Called to Coach*
and *Heisman: The Man Behind the Trophy*

THE WARREN OMISSIONS

"What can be more fascinating than a super high concept novel that reopens the conspiracy behind the JFK assassination while the threat of a global world war rests in the balance? With his new novel, *The Warren Omissions*, former journalist turned bestselling author R.J. Patterson proves he just might be the next worthy successor to Vince Flynn."
- ***Vincent Zandri***
bestselling author of THE REMAINS

OTHER TITLES BY R.J. PATTERSON

Titus Black Thrillers
Behind Enemy Lines
Game of Shadows
Rogue Commander
Line of Fire

James Flynn Thrillers
The Warren Omissions
Imminent Threat
The Cooper Affair
Seeds of War

Brady Hawk Thrillers
First Strike
Deep Cover
Point of Impact
Full Blast
Target Zero
Fury
State of Play
Siege
Seek and Destroy
Into the Shadows
Hard Target
No Way Out
Two Minutes to Midnight
Against All Odds
Amy Means Necessary
Vengeance
Code Red
A Deadly Force
Divide and Conquer
Extreme Measures
Final Strike

DIVIDE AND CONQUER

A Brady Hawk novel

R.J. PATTERSON

DIVIDE AND CONQUER
© Copyright 2019 R.J. Patterson

This novel is a work of fiction. Names, characters, places, and incidents either are the product of the author's imagination or are used fictitiously. Any resemblance to actual persons, living or dead, events, or locales is entirely coincidental.

First Print Edition 2021

All rights reserved. No part of this book may be reproduced or transmitted in any form or by any means, electronic or mechanical, including photocopying, recording, or by any information storage and retrieval system, without the written permission of the Publisher, except where permitted by law.

Cover Design by Books Covered

Published in the United States of America
Green E-Books
Boise Idaho 83713

For Paul Ragan, from storming the beaches of Normandy to showing me how to throw a knuckle ball, you were one amazing man who I still miss deeply.

CHAPTER 1

12°09'28.5"S 96°49'41.2"E
Cocos Islands
Indian Ocean

BRADY HAWK WORMED HIS WAY across the sand, taking cover beneath the shrubbery growing about ten feet up the shore. A cool breeze brought a respite from the late afternoon heat typical on most tropical islands. He glanced at his watch and then peered through his binoculars at the designated meeting spot. No one had shown up yet.

"Is he there?" Alex asked over the coms.

"No sign of him," Hawk said. "But he isn't late yet."

"In one more minute, he will be," she said. "And this isn't exactly the kind of place we can go charging into and inquiring about his whereabouts."

Hawk sighed and shook his head, still keeping his eyes trained on the meeting spot, which was about twenty meters away on the shore of a small shaded inlet.

Alex was right, and he felt helpless to do anything about it.

Two days earlier, Hawk and Alex were meeting with their boss, Phoenix Foundation director J.D. Blunt, when he received a message from one of his back channel protocols set up when the organization was known as Firestorm. Blunt still kept them open just in case a friend of the group ever needed help. According to Blunt, no one had ever utilized the open line of communication—until now.

The asset's name was Tyler Timmons, a former engineer at Colton Industries who worked several covert projects with Blunt's team before disappearing four years ago. His car was found abandoned near the Hoover Dam along with a note saying he was sorry but he just couldn't go on any more. Local law enforcement officials didn't discover any signs of foul play and wrote it off as a suicide. Even Blunt had assumed suicide was the logical explanation. However, Timmons's message changed Blunt's mind.

Timmons reported that he had some information that was vital to national security, but he needed to be extracted from a remote island in the Indian Ocean. He warned Blunt about the facility's tight security and suggested that they meet at a location accessible from the interior of the island with a quick escape route back to the water.

Hawk and Alex had arrived the day before on Blunt's private jet, posing as researchers gathering information on the unique ecology of the atoll. They rented a boat and collected approved samples, all while secretly scouting the best exit strategy from the portion of the island where they were to meet Timmons. Once Hawk and Alex secured the engineer, they'd need to get to the airport on the southwestern portion of the atoll and leave immediately.

Everything was in place to carry out the extraction except for one thing: Timmons.

"It's a minute past noon," Alex said. "Is this guy coming or not?"

"Still nothing," Hawk said.

"The longer this goes, the more I'm starting to feel like this is a trap."

"Just be patient."

Hawk scanned the area once more and noticed movement through the bushes on the other side of the inlet.

"Hold on," Hawk said.

"Is it him?"

Hawk squinted, trying to make out the source of the activity in the brush. When the image became clearer, he sighed.

"It's just a bird," he said.

"I say we get out of here," she said. "We don't

want to be compromised. If he didn't think he could make it to the designated location on time, he should've told us so somehow."

"I agree," Hawk said. "But I don't want to abandon him just yet."

"You're a saint, honey. But I'm getting more worried as each minute ticks past."

A rustling in the bushes arrested Hawk's attention. He placed his binoculars up to his eyes and searched the forest just on the other side of the water one final time.

No bird sounds like that running through the woods.

"Get the boat ready," Hawk said over his coms as he stood and met Timmons's gaze. "I've got the asset."

"Roger that," she said, followed by the sound of the boat engine roaring to life in the background.

As Timmons raced along the shore, he shook his head, eyes wide with fear.

"Move it," he shouted.

Hawk didn't wait for a second plea, spinning on his heels and dashing into the forest. Timmons had almost caught up with Hawk before a hail of bullets rained down on their position. Without hesitating, he dove to the ground.

Timmons, however, staggered to the forest floor, collapsing face down in a pile of leaves.

"Stay with me," Hawk said as he rolled Timmons over.

"They're coming," Timmons said, holding up his hand. "There's no time."

Hawk helped Timmons to his feet. "I'll get you out of here."

The back of Timmons's shirt soaked up blood leaking from the bullet wound about three inches below his shoulder blade. Timmons staggered to his feet and limped forward.

After they jogged a few feet, Timmons crashed to the ground again, this time landing on his knees.

"I can't do it," he said as he gasped for air. "They'll catch us both if you don't go on."

"Who's *they*?" Hawk asked.

Timmons dug into his pocket and handed Black a flash drive. "Obsidian. It's all on there, but it's encrypted."

"What's the password?" Hawk asked.

Before Timmons could say another word, a barrage of bullets peppered nearby. Hawk hit the ground.

"I'm gonna get you out of here," Hawk said.

He turned and looked at Timmons, who was bleeding from a shot to the head.

Hawk let out a string of expletives before scrambling to his feet and racing through the woods.

"I'm coming," Hawk said over the coms. "And I'm coming alone."

"Alone?"

"Timmons is dead—and I've got some security personnel on my tail."

"How many?" she asked.

"I have no idea. Just get the boat ready because we're going to need to leave immediately."

Hawk hit the beach thirty seconds later and sprinted up to the dock. He didn't look back as he raced across the wooden planks, waving his arms at Alex.

"I hope you're ready to go," he said.

She cursed as she stared in his direction.

"What is it?" Hawk said, refusing to glance over his shoulder.

"There are three hostiles, and one of them has a rocket launcher," she said. "Hurry."

Alex ripped the rope off the cleat and hustled back to the wheel where she slammed the accelerator forward. The boat lurched as the propellers churned through the water.

Hawk leaped off the end of the dock just as the boat started to gain momentum. He slammed hard against the side but managed to hang onto the railing before throwing himself inside. He rolled back over and pulled his gun, providing Alex with the cover she needed to guide the boat farther out to sea and out of harm's way.

However, Hawk couldn't do anything about the man with the rocket launcher foisted onto his shoulder.

"Alex," Hawk shouted.

Alex glanced over her shoulder. "I see him."

"Just keep driving," Hawk said. "When he fires, bank hard in the direction I tell you. Got it?"

"Roger that."

Hawk took a few more shots at the guards before he ran out of bullets. Then a flash of fire erupted from the man holding the launcher. Hawk had to decide quickly which side of the boat the missile was most likely to strike.

"Left," Hawk yelled as the incoming missile appeared poised to strike the starboard side.

He gripped the railing as Alex yanked the wheel hard. The boat slowed for a moment as it turned toward the port side then picked up speed as the nose rose. With Alex pushing the throttle to the limit, the vessel sped through the calm waters surrounding the atoll.

If the brief gunfight hadn't garnered the attention from locals on the shores, the explosion surely did, igniting a flurry of activity as people raced to the water's edge to see what was happening.

"Is the pilot ready?" Hawk asked.

"He was supposed to be ready to take off five minutes ago," Alex said. "But I guess we're about to find out."

Alex ran the boat aground, and the two agents hustled off it before breaking into a dead run across the shore toward the quiet airport.

"Where is he?" Hawk asked as he stared at the plane sitting on the rudimentary tarmac without the engines on. The steps were unfurled, but Hawk felt uneasy.

"Damn it. I told him to be ready, no excuses."

Hawk surveyed the scene and tried to determine how to approach it. He stopped and grabbed Alex by her arm.

"Wait," he said. "I've got another idea."

* * *

HAWK EASED AROUND the front of the plane, assessing the situation. If the pilot wasn't on board, he was in serious breach of protocol, never mind that he didn't adhere to the directives to have the plane running and ready for takeoff.

"Kip," Hawk called, "are you in there?"

Seconds later, their pilot, Kip Covington, appeared at the doorway with a gun jammed into his head by a bald man with a pair of dark sunglasses.

"Where is it?" the man asked.

"Whoa, whoa," Hawk said, raising his hands in the air. "What are you talking about? Where's what?"

"The device that Timmons gave you," the man in the sunglasses said with a growl.

"Timmons? Who's that?" Hawk said. "I'm afraid you have me mixed up with someone else. I'm just a researcher from San Diego State's PhD ecology program here to collect some tropical plant specimens."

"Do I look stupid to you?" the man sneered. "Now, where is it?"

"You're more than welcome to check my pockets for whatever you're looking for," Hawk said. "But I'm sure whatever you find there, you'll be able to find anywhere here along the beach."

"If you don't want your pilot dead, I'm giving you five seconds to place the device on the ground and back away."

"Fine," Hawk said. "You win." He knelt and emptied his pockets onto the tarmac.

The man grabbed Kip by the collar, ushering him to the items Hawk had just piled up.

"Grab the flash drive," the man ordered.

Kip's hands shook as he sifted through the stuff. He winced when a gunshot pierced the air. A second later, his captor collapsed.

"Nice shot," Hawk said with a grin on his face.

Alex hustled up next to the man and stepped on his wrist, pinning it to the ground, before kicking the gun out of his hand. She knelt and checked his pulse.

"He's gone," she said. "What are we going to do about him?"

"Just take the body with us," Kip said. "We'll dump him somewhere over the Indian Ocean."

Hawk looked at his pilot. "Are you okay?"

Kip shook his head.

"Can you still fly us out of here?" Alex asked.

"Anything to get off this god-forsaken island."

"Well, let's not waste any more time," Hawk said. "We don't want to be detained and questioned by anyone."

The trio worked to get the hostile's body on board and into the cargo hold. Kip said he'd already gone through all his checks and had the plane idling before the man accosted him. In less than five minutes, Kip had them airborne and soaring over the remote atoll.

Meanwhile, Alex didn't wait long to pull out her laptop and begin her quest to crack open the flash drive. She hammered away at the keys on her computer while Hawk waited anxiously.

"How's it looking?" Hawk asked.

She sighed as she hung her head.

"What's the matter?" he pressed. "Did he not give us the right drive?"

"No, we got the right device, all right," she said. "It just uses an RSA 4096 bit encryption key."

"I'm guessing by the look on your face that you can't crack it."

"Me and a legion of NSA decoders probably wouldn't be able to get into these files."

"So this was a dead end for us?"

She shook her head. "Not yet. A situation like this just requires a little creativity."

"What kind of creativity?" he asked.

"The kind that requires us to dabble in the dark side."

Hawk's eyebrows shot upward. "Black hat hacker?"

"Bingo," she said, pointing at him.

"And I'm hoping you know where to find one of these computing experts."

"Of course," she said. "I know just the guy to handle this."

CHAPTER 2

Washington, D.C.

BLUNT STOOD ON the corner of Constitution and 7th, waiting for his ride. Ever since he received the horrifying text message containing the image of his niece bound and gagged, Blunt wondered who might be attempting to blackmail him. When he responded, he learned nothing of his niece's tormentor. The person responding said that they needed to connect in person before specifying the details for their meeting, which they would send later in the week and provide only thirty minutes to reach a street corner in Washington near his office where he would be picked up in a limousine. No cell phones would be allowed, and he would be swept for bugs and trackers after getting inside.

Blunt didn't like the terms, but he had no choice. Morgan was his sister's only child, now a twenty-four-year-old woman finishing up her master's degree in international business just down the road at the University of Virginia. She aimed to enter the CIA's Clandestine Service Program after getting a job overseas for a couple of years, a plan that Blunt tried—and failed—to dissuade her from pursuing.

The fact that someone found out about Blunt's relation to Morgan angered him. He'd been careful to prevent any link from being made through online documentation, including family photos and ancestry websites. He only had one photo of her that he took with an old camera that required film development when she was eight. But somebody had managed to figure out who she was and connected the dots, resulting in an exploitation that put her at risk. Blunt could only imagine who was behind it, much less what would be demanded of him.

When the limo pulled up to the curb, a burly man stepped out and frisked Blunt. Once they were both inside the car, the man checked Blunt for any electronic devices.

"Strictly a precautionary measure," the man said. "We must make sure that everyone adheres to our stipulations."

"*Our?*" Blunt asked, cocking his head to one side.

The man clasped his hands together, resting them in his lap and staring straight ahead.

"You may proceed," he said, refusing to answer

Blunt's obvious question.

The car eased into Washington traffic and drove for several minutes until it parked beneath an overpass. Once the vehicle came to a stop, Blunt's door flung open and another man greeted him by pointing at the limo behind him.

Blunt slid out and trudged to the other vehicle. He didn't get in until he watched two identical limousines depart in opposite directions at the same time while his remained stationary.

"Get in," came a soft voice from inside.

Blunt hunched down and peered inside, his gaze locking with that of a young woman, who couldn't have been much older than thirty, if that.

"Mr. Blunt," she said in an accent that he wasn't quite convinced originated in England, "we appreciate you agreeing to meet with us."

"You didn't give me much choice," Blunt said with a snarl.

"Unfortunately, we must apply the necessary pressure to ensure that you agree to work with us."

"And who is this *us* you're speaking of?" Blunt asked.

"My name is Elizabeth Silverstone, and I work for a very powerful organization," she began. "Perhaps you've heard of Obsidian?"

Blunt glared at her. "So, this is how you do it?

Exploit everyone's relationships and force them to do your bidding?"

She shrugged. "Sometimes you can't ignore a proven method, no matter how barbaric it might seem at the time."

"I get it," he said. "Results matter."

"And that's precisely why we chose to work with you for this particular project," she said. "All our past intelligence reports have shown that you have the president's ear—and that he listens to you."

"I'm not sure what this is all about, but I can assure you that I'm only an advisor to the president. He pretty much does whatever he very well pleases. If you think I'm going to whisper in his ear and steer him to do what you desire, I'm afraid you're making a grave mistake."

"How so?"

"President Young doesn't like anyone to tell him what to do," Blunt said. "He's very much a maverick in that respect."

"In that case, we expect you to be a good Texas rancher and corral him."

"And how am I supposed to do that?"

"It's simple, really," she said. "All we want you to do is get someone on the guest list for the First Lady's funeral later this week. We understand from media reports that she won't be lying in state due to her disfigured nature suffered in the explosion."

Elizabeth smiled slyly before closing her eyes. When she opened them again, Blunt had narrowed his and pursed his lips.

"This was a complete set up, wasn't it?" he asked.

"I'm not sure what you're suggesting, Mr. Blunt, but I do know that my employer demands that you acquiesce to the terms of this arrangement or else face severe consequences, dare I say, *fatal* consequences."

"And just who is this person?"

"I'm not at liberty to reveal that to you," she said. "All I'm asking is that you deliver this envelope to President Young. It will also be up to you to persuade him to comply with the request."

"Do I even need to run this past him?" Blunt asked.

"That's up to you, but I'd advise you to select the path of least resistance," she said. "In my experience, I've discovered that things always work better that way."

She handed him an envelope. "Don't open it. Just give that to the appropriate people and let them finish the task for you. Your niece will be most grateful that you did."

"You know I'm going to find out who's behind this," Blunt said.

"I'm sure you will, but I'd caution you against

reacting in a rash manner," she said, wagging her finger. "Sometimes when we jump to conclusions, we make grave mistakes."

"Are you threatening me?"

Elizabeth chuckled and waved dismissively at Blunt. "Dear one, you're already being threatened. We know how much you adore your niece, which is why you'll do exactly as we say. Now run along."

"Run along?"

"Yes, there's a car waiting for you outside to take you back to the same place we picked you up."

Blunt looked down at the envelope and then back at Elizabeth. "Someone is going to pay for this."

"Your niece will be the one paying the price if you don't pass that envelope along to the right person and secure my employer a spot at the First Lady's funeral. Is that understood?"

Blunt didn't say a word, responding only with a grunt. He climbed out of the vehicle and found a taxi waiting for him. He opened the door and watched as the two other limos returned before all leaving together in a caravan.

Blunt cursed under his breath before getting into the cab and slamming the door shut.

"I've been instructed to take you to the corner of Constitution and 7th," the driver said as he looked in the rearview mirror at Blunt. "Is that correct?"

Blunt nodded. He eased back in his seat and buckled himself in. Then he slid his finger beneath the flap of the envelope, breaking the seal. If he was going to be blackmailed, he wanted to who was victimizing him.

When he saw the name on the paper, he stared stoically at it. He wasn't surprised at all.

That's who I knew was behind this.

He sighed and then read the name aloud with a hint of disgust: "Falcon Sinclair."

CHAPTER 3

Washington, D.C.

WHEN HAWK AND ALEX returned to The Phoenix Foundation headquarters, they found Blunt gnawing on a cigar and pacing around his office. His gaze was affixed on a document in his hands, lines creasing his forehead.

"Reading the latest stock market report?" Hawk asked.

Blunt looked up over his reading glasses and sneered. "Don't get me started about my IRA. But it's nothing compared to this."

"Latest Homeland Security briefing?" Alex asked.

"A scathing rebuke of the intelligence community for allowing the attack on the White House," Blunt said as he gestured for Hawk and Alex to sit in the two chairs across from his desk.

"When both the White House and the FBI has been infiltrated by multiple assets, it's difficult to avoid an attack like this," she said.

Blunt nodded as he sank into his chair and flung down his papers. "That doesn't mean somebody's head isn't going to roll over this. But there's nothing we can do about what's happened. The question for us is how are we going to stop this from happening again?"

"We're working on it," Hawk said.

Blunt sighed. "What happened at the Cocos?"

"Sorry about Tyler Timmons, sir," Alex said. "We know that he was more than just someone who worked for you."

"Thanks," Blunt said. "I appreciate that. His father and I were friends for years. I was the one that steered Timmons into this line of work, and I can't help but shoulder some of the responsibility for his death."

Hawk leaned forward in his seat. "No, sir. Don't go there. This wasn't your fault. Timmons wanted out, and he reached out to you. If we would've just had more time—"

The silence that hung in the room after Blunt trailed off weighed heavily on Hawk. "Obsidian obviously has something big planned. I mean, whatever it is, Timmons was willing to sacrifice his life for it. I'm sure he knew the risks. In fact, I'm not convinced that he necessarily expected to escape."

"What makes you say that?" Blunt asked.

Hawk leaned back in his chair. "For one thing, the flash drive is heavily encrypted, protecting anyone who got caught with it, himself included."

"From what you told me about the incident, it doesn't sound like anyone gave him an opportunity to explain himself, did they?"

Hawk shook his head. "The Obsidian guards certainly weren't attempting to make a capture. And based on the fact that they were firing rockets at us, they weren't interested in questioning us either."

"So, what's the status of the decryption?" Blunt asked. "Anything yet?"

Alex shook her head. "I reached out to a couple of local people first, but neither one of them think they can crack it within a month."

Blunt's jaw fell slack. "A month? I don't think we have that kind of time."

"I agree, sir, which is why we need to go a different route," Alex said.

"I'm listening," Blunt said. "But why do I have the feeling I'm not going to like this?"

"Just keep an open mind," she said.

"I can tell you right now the answer is going to be no."

"The only hacker I know who can handle a job like this in a timely manner is Helenos-9."

Blunt shook his head emphatically. "Absolutely not. Out of the question."

"But, sir—"

"No," Blunt continued. "He penetrated all the Pentagon's firewalls and started distributing names of our assets. He's certainly not a friend of the U.S. government, and I wouldn't trust his intel as far as I could throw him."

Alex cocked her head to one side. "There's nobody else who has his expertise. We can't afford to be bullheaded if Obsidian is about to launch an attack that threatens the security of this country and maybe others as well."

Blunt bit down hard on his cigar and then pulled it out of his mouth. "How do we know that he's not already in Obsidian's pocket? They've been so many steps ahead of us at every turn that I'm reticent to turn over the one piece of intel we have."

"Sir, it's a chance we have to take if we expect to snuff out their plot," Alex said.

"She's right. According to every intelligence report I've read, the world is a tinderbox right now. And if Obsidian tosses a spark into the mix, it's going to explode. If we sit on this and something happens, we're no better off than if we give it to Helenos-9 and he betrays us. We'll only have ourselves to blame for inaction. We can't wait out what Obsidian is doing."

"The problem is we don't even really know what they're planning to do yet," Blunt said.

"We know enough to know that whatever they are plotting is going to compromise our security and put thousands, if not millions, at risk," Hawk said. "I mean, this is why we do what we do. We make the hard calls, appearances be damned. People are counting on us to keep them safe, and we can't do that by hoping for the best."

Blunt stood and began pacing around the room. "I know you're right. It's just that sometimes these decisions can be multi-layered and more complicated than they seem."

Hawk eyed his boss closely. "They haven't gotten to you, have they?"

Blunt drew back and scowled. "Of course not. Why would you even suggest such a thing?"

"I don't know," Hawk said. "Usually you're a bit more decisive than this."

"Helenos-9 has burned me in the past," Blunt said. "I'm just a little hesitant to put any trust in him."

"He's the best," Alex said. "If there was anyone else—"

Blunt sighed. "I know, I know. Okay, fine. Go find him and see if he's willing to help us."

"If I know Helenos-9, he's going to ask us to expunge the charges against him," she said. "Do you have the authority to do that?"

"Don't worry. I'll get that cleared with Randy

Wood at the CIA. If we're desperate enough to reach out to him, we have to be willing to make some concessions. Now, are you sure you can find him?"

Alex nodded. "I have a girlfriend who used to date him. I know where he hangs out."

"You should've told me about that earlier," Blunt said.

"Hackers code," she said with a wink.

"Go on," Blunt said. "Get outta here. Report back as soon as you know something."

"Roger that," Hawk said.

"Good luck at the First Lady's funeral," Alex said.

Blunt furrowed his brow. "Good luck? Why would I need luck?"

"You're a terrible actor," she said. "Just try your best to keep a somber face."

"I'll show you my angry face if you don't get moving."

"Your resting face is your angry face," Alex quipped.

Blunt shook his finger at her. "I'm warning you, Alex. You're going to make me really mad in a minute."

Hawk took Alex by the wrist and gave her a gentle tug. "Let's go, dear."

She followed him out of the room, and they headed toward the exit.

"You think something's up with Blunt?" she asked in a hushed tone.

"Without a doubt," Hawk said. "I just don't know what yet."

* * *

BLUNT SHUT THE DOOR to his office and then fished his cell phone out of his pocket. He dialed a number and waited for someone to answer.

"Well done," the man said as he answered the phone. "Your niece will be home before you know it."

"I did what you asked," Blunt said. "Now, where can I pick her up?"

"You didn't think it was that simple, did you? The first part of your assignment was to secure an invitation to the First Lady's funeral this afternoon."

"*First part?*" Blunt asked. "Nobody ever mentioned anything about becoming an errand boy for Falcon Sinclair."

The man clucked his tongue. "You looked at the invitation, Mr. Blunt. You're a bad boy."

"You ain't seen nothing yet."

"What was that?" the man asked.

"I said—"

Sounds of Morgan screaming made Blunt stop mid-sentence.

When her cries of pain stopped, the man continued. "Now, what were you saying again, Mr. Blunt?"

"Let her go," Blunt said. "She's done nothing to deserve this."

"You're right. She hasn't. But you have. Now the sooner you cease with the empty threats, the sooner we can establish a better understanding of how this relationship is going to work moving forward. I have people give you orders, and then you do them. Understand?"

Blunt seethed as he stared out his window, refusing to answer.

"Perhaps you didn't hear me, Mr. Blunt. Do you understand?" the man asked again.

"Yeah," Blunt muttered.

"Good. Now that we've cleared that up, you're going to do what we tell you to do, and you're not going to complain about it."

"Or what?"

"Do I really need to spell it out for you? You're a smart man, Mr. Blunt. You know what'll happen."

Blunt hung up and resisted the urge to kick his trash can across the room. He strode over to the mirror and studied his weathered face.

"Think I look angry now, just you wait."

CHAPTER 4

Washington, D.C.

FALCON SINCLAIR DUG HIS Patek Philippe Calibre 89 pocket watch out of his suit vest to check the time. His Airbus ACJ319 jet came to a halt as he calculated that he would have just about five minutes to spare in reaching the First Lady's funeral if the city's traffic didn't become more snarled than usual. Due to the number of dignitaries attending the service for Madeline Young, congestion at Washington National meant his pilot had to spend an extra half hour circling the airport. His extravagant wealth bought him plenty, but apparently it couldn't compete with the power of important American politicians.

"Alfred," Sinclair said in his thick Aussie accent, "change of plans."

"What would you like me to do, sir?" asked the genteel septuagenarian who'd spent the past five decades serving the Sinclair family.

"Without the motorcade, we're going to need an alternate form of transportation to the service."

"Again, I'm sorry, sir, that we weren't able to arrange that beforehand. Working on such short notice along with the apparent large influx of VIPs attending the First Lady's funeral created obstacles that were too much for us to overcome."

"It happens," Sinclair said. "But nothing a short helicopter ride won't remedy."

"Sir, I already considered that," Alfred said. "I just couldn't find a place to land."

Sinclair sighed. "Alfred, when are you going to catch up with the times? I swear, I might as well let you go since I have to do everything myself around here these days. I'll make a donation to the St. Albans School just a block away, and they'll let us use their athletic fields to land the helicopter."

"I'm terribly sorry, sir. I just thought that—"

"It's all right, old chap," Sinclair said. "I'll just take a portion of that gift money from the generous salary I give you. But trust me when I say that if my father hadn't been so kind to you when he endowed you a job until the end of your life, I would've moved on a long time ago."

"I understand, sir. You remind me of that daily."

Sinclair rested his head in his right hand and sighed. "Sadly, it's a point that bears repeating. Do better."

Sinclair relied upon Selena, his perky twenty-five-year-old assistant, to handle most of his transportation requests. But she was getting married in less than a week and had requested time off months in advance. If she had been any other employee, he would've demanded that she work, wedding be damned. But she was different. They had a special relationship, the kind that he went to great lengths to keep from his wife and two other mistresses. Selena had promised him that nothing would change after she got married, an arrangement that made him abnormally forgiving of her absence at such a critical juncture in the overall timeline of his plan. Having to rely upon Alfred to arrange transportation concerned Sinclair, but not to the point that he was overly worried. The kind of power he'd only dreamed of was within reach once a few more pieces fell into place. Complete command was so close now it was almost palpable. And the last thing he wanted was a little traffic jam to delay his scheme—or possibly thwart it all together.

Sinclair happened to meet the headmaster at the St. Albans School, Valentine Prescott, at a fundraiser for endangered marine life in Sydney just a few months earlier. Their conversation had been a pleasant one, though brief, and consisted of their shared joy of snorkeling. But based on the way Prescott hemmed and hawed over the request to land on the St. Albans athletic fields, Sinclair concluded that he hadn't made the kind of impression that immediately endeared him to the school's director.

When they hung up, Sinclair pointed at Alfred and smiled. "There's not much a generous one million dollar donation won't solve."

"Are you ready to move, sir?" Alfred asked.

"Did you get clearance for us to utilize the airspace over the city?"

Alfred nodded. "There will be another fifty thousand dollars required for the White House official who grants such clearance. I trust that you're prepared to meet such demands."

"Of course," Sinclair said. "That's a bargain for sure, Alfred. I may not even charge you for the difference in what it costs for me to rent a helicopter."

"Thank you, sir," Alfred said. "That's most kind."

Sinclair rolled his eyes.

Nothing like a tenured butler.

* * *

A HALF HOUR LATER, Sinclair ducked as he exited the heli taxi and hustled across the St. Albans School athletics field. He waved at the boys crowded along the fence, many of them staring slack-jawed at the Australian billionaire. Hustling toward the sidewalk,

Sinclair found a limousine waiting by the curb, complete with a gloved driver standing by an open door.

"Are we going to make it on time?" Sinclair asked, buttoning his jacket as he approached the vehicle.

"Without question, sir," the man said. "However, I won't be able to get you up to the steps due to the security protocol. You'll have to cross the street at the corner. I trust that won't inconvenience you too much."

Sinclair nodded. "I understand. It's the price of safety in this day and age."

He eased inside and slid across the seat. Once his door was closed, the driver strode around to the front and made exactly two turns before he reached the unloading zone.

Sinclair tipped the man and crossed the street.

Once inside the church, he wove through the sea of diplomats and dignitaries, all on hand to pay their last respects to Madeline Young. Sinclair knew most of the people on hand had never even met the First Lady. Not that he was intimately acquainted with her either. He'd spoken with her on two different occasions, both times expressing her dissatisfaction with the leadership of her husband. He explained that there were other options, which piqued her interest—and eventually persuaded her to volunteer to help.

Sinclair resisted the urge to smile as he approached the front door where photographers swarmed like a hive of hornets deliberating over their next victim. He knew Madeline Young wasn't dead, but he needed to at least give the appearance of someone who was saddened by her passing. From what he'd seen on television, even President Young seemed convinced that his wife had passed away in the attack.

After forking over his invitation to one of the secret service agents, a man waved his wand around the sleek contours of Sinclair's body. Once the guard was finished, he gestured for Sinclair to go into the sanctuary, satisfied that he wasn't a threat to anyone.

And at a cursory glance, the guard was right. But Sinclair was determined to parlay his invite into an event that disrupted the world's power structure.

Once the funeral began, Sinclair sat restlessly through several homages of people who were sharing stories about the public face of Madeline Young— kind, amicable, classy. But Sinclair had heard otherwise from others working closely with her. Behind closed doors, she was a monster, sharp-tongued and not a fan of her husband's policies. And according to one staffer, she wasn't happy with her husband in general, not to mention that she had a reputation among the Secret Service for carrying on a potentially scandalous dalliance or two. Her penchant for such relationships inspired his plan to have the late General Fortner woo her, a suggestion that didn't need much encouragement given how gorgeous the First Lady was. She wasn't Sinclair's type, but she seemed to be more than desirable to most men, and he leveraged that into Obsidian's infiltration of the White House bedroom. But Sinclair's plan was far from finished.

He pulled out his pocket watch again, checking the time. An hour had elapsed since the funeral started, and the eulogies began to sound all alike.

Once the service finally ended, Sinclair joined a procession with President Young and his invited friends and family to the graveside service. Without any cell phones allowed and only one pool photographer for the press, Sinclair saw the opportunity to connect with the president without prying eyes. Sinclair was prepared to issue an invitation that Young would be inclined to receive with just the right pitch. And since Sinclair had already engineered the compelling reason that would stir the president's emotions, acceptance was a mere formality.

As Madeline Young's casket and faked remains were lowered into the ground, Young stood by the graveside, head bowed and hands clasped in front of him. His tear-stained cheeks shook as his soft crying transitioned to wailing.

Sinclair decided to seize the moment of grief and

approached Young. A Secret Service agent slid in front of Sinclair and put a hand to his chest followed by a subtle shake of his head.

"Give him a moment," the agent said.

"Of course," Sinclair replied, backing away.

After another minute, the man looked at Sinclair and nodded at him before gesturing toward Young.

Sinclair strode up to the president and put his arm around him. "I'm so sorry for your loss, sir."

Young looked up and turned toward Sinclair, their eyes locking. "Did you know my wife?"

Sinclair shook his head. "Unfortunately, our paths never crossed. And based off all I heard today, since she's gone makes that fact an even sadder one."

"She was a big fan of all your space exploration," Young said, his dour countenance lightening as he recalled his wife's enthusiasm for space travel. "I don't know how many times she implored me to direct NASA to restart the shuttle program and take more trips into space. I think deep down she thought she might be able to sneak on a future mission as a pilot."

The two men began walking toward the line of waiting vehicles.

"I was certainly aware of her passion for space exploration," Sinclair said.

"Well, I appreciate you coming to pay your last respects to a woman you never even met. I know it likely wasn't easy for you to get here so quickly, but I was pleased to hear from my staff that you were interested in attending today."

"It's the least I can do."

"Is there something more you'd like to do?"

Sinclair nodded. "As a matter of fact, there is. I know that you're still grieving over your wife's death, but you shouldn't be. The only reason we're standing here is because of another violent act from someone determined to inflict pain on you personally as well as instill more fear into the American people."

"And there's little we can do about it, especially when the world is teeming with terrorists intent on raining down death and destruction on our country. We do what we can, but it's difficult to fight a foe with nothing to lose."

"Until now," Sinclair said. "My team has engineered a new weapon that might help you turn the table on terrorists and make them fear you like never before. Interested?"

Young stopped, his eyebrows shooting upward as he cocked his head to one side. "Very much so."

"Excellent," Sinclair said. "Next week, I'll be conducting a private demonstration that I would love for you to see for yourself. I'll send your office all the details."

Young offered his hand to Sinclair, which he took.

"I'll look forward to it."

"We'll put an end to this era of fear in our world," Sinclair said. "Good day, Mr. President."

Sinclair resisted the urge to smile as he strode toward his limousine. However, when he reached the door, J.D. Blunt was waiting for him, leaning against the side of the vehicle and chewing on a cigar.

"Mr. Sinclair, what a surprise," Blunt said. "I had no idea you were even acquainted with the First Lady."

Sinclair stroked his chin. "Surprised? I hardly believe that since you helped secure this invitation for me."

"I don't trust people who struggle with sarcasm."

"That's the difference between you and me," Sinclair said. "I don't trust anyone."

"Whatever your end game is, I advise you to leave President Young out of it. He's not to be messed with."

"And how are you going to stop him whenever he decides that partnering with me is in the best interest of his country? A coup? A revolt? I advise you to stay in your lane. Now, if you'll excuse me, I have business elsewhere that I need to attend to."

Blunt didn't budge. "No, you have some business with me that needs your attention right now." He held out his cell phone. "Call that number and give the order for my niece to be released."

Sinclair furrowed his brow. "Why would I do that?"

"I upheld my end of the bargain."

"I don't bargain, Mr. Blunt. I command. And when we're done, you'll get your precious niece back."

"So help me, when I—"

"I'd stop right there if I were you," Sinclair said. "I've found that nothing makes a man look weaker than issuing empty threats. And I doubt you want to appear any weaker than you already do."

Blunt glanced around to make sure no one was looking at them. Satisfied that their conversation was private, he pulled back his jacket revealing his gun and glanced at it.

"Another empty threat," Sinclair said. "You're weak, and you'll never get this close to me ever again."

He pushed his way past Blunt and stepped inside the limo. "When President Young accepts my invitation, I'll release your niece if I'm in a generous mood when I receive the news. If not, I might hold on to her for a few days just for fun. Good day, Mr. Blunt."

Sinclair pulled the door shut and exhaled. He picked up his phone and dialed a number.

"I need someone to watch Mr. Blunt," Sinclair said. "He's going to be more trouble than I first thought."

CHAPTER 5

Berlin, Germany

HAWK PULLED HIS HOOD over his head and tugged on the drawstrings. He took Alex's hands as they strolled along casually. The Spree River flowed gently through the center of the city, creating an interesting juxtaposition between the serene water and the bustling metropolis. Even at 1:30 a.m., Berlin was abuzz with activity.

As they veered down Köpenicker Street toward Tresor nightclub, Hawk could already feel the pulsating base rhythms vibrating in his chest. He took a deep breath and caught a whiff of cigarette smoke mixed with marijuana. They strode toward the entrance, passing several couples engaged in unashamed makeout sessions.

"How can someone who watches Bollywood movies enjoy visiting this kind of dance club?" Hawk asked.

Alex smiled and winked at him. "Work assignments."

"All of a sudden, that raises all kinds of questions."

She yanked on his arm and dragged him toward the door. "Come on," she said. "I promise not to make you dance. Just let me do all the talking here. And put on your sunglasses, okay?"

Hawk nodded and complied with her requests. He remained silent while studying the club's clientele.

They waited in line for ten minutes before reaching the door of the three-story industrial building that used to be a heating plant, according to Alex. The bouncer at the door had a shaved head except for a strip of spiked hair, proudly displaying the intricate symbol tattooed across his brow.

"Who are you here to see?" the man asked in German.

"My favorite DJ, False Witness," Alex responded in crisp German.

The man eyed Hawk. "And what about him?"

"He's with me and a little too stoned to talk."

The bouncer held out his hand. "Twenty Euros each."

Alex forked over the cash and rushed inside before the man changed his mind.

"What was that all about?" Hawk asked.

"These clubs are notorious for discriminating at

the door, oftentimes for no good reason. And if you're American or British, your chances of getting inside aren't great, even on a night when the bouncers are feeling generous."

"Did you ever get turned away?"

"Bouncers are like cops," she said. "Just bat your eyes and make a sad puppy dog face. Works every time I get in pinch."

Hawk rolled his eyes. "Can you use your superpower to find Helenos-9 so we can get out of here?"

"What? I thought we might stay and dance some."

Hawk shook his head. "This isn't my scene."

She drew back. "Why not? I've already seen at least three people sporting cowboy boots."

"You're not nearly as funny as you think you are."

Alex chuckled. "Follow me."

She led Hawk up to the bar where she called for the bartender.

"Peter," she said.

He turned around, and his eyes widened as soon as he recognized her. "Alex? Is that you?"

She nodded. "In the flesh."

"You're an angelic apparition," he said. "I never thought I'd see you again."

"Well, here I am."

"Yes, you are," Peter said as he cut his eyes over at Hawk. "And who's this?"

"This is my boyfriend, Carlos."

"Oh, Carlos, what a lucky man you are," Peter said. "Alex is fabulous."

Hawk nodded. "I'm starting to believe that's the case."

Peter turned toward Alex. "What are you doing back here?"

"I need a little help."

"With what?"

Alex glanced around the room before looking back at Peter. "Have you seen Ian tonight?"

"Oh, he's in the back corner up there," he said, pointing at the third floor. "But better catch him before he has too many more drinks in him."

"Of course," she said, wasting no more time talking and hustling away from the bar. "Good to see you, Peter."

"Wait, I wanted to—"

His voice vanished in a sea of conversations muted by the pulsating rhythms of techno mix.

Hawk leaned forward and spoke loudly in Alex's ear. "Carlos? Really? I thought you'd come up with something a little more appropriate than that."

She smiled and shook her head. "Be glad I didn't go with something less imposing like Melvin."

"I don't really care," Hawk said. "But seriously, what was that all about at the bar with Peter?"

"It's nothing. He's a nosy character, so I wanted to get out of there before he started grilling you. He's rather protective of me in a big brother kind of way."

They hustled up the steps and strode over to Ian, the infamous Helenos-9 when he was online. He wore a white polo with his collar popped up and a pair of sunglasses. When he stood to greet Alex, Hawk was struck by just how short the hacker was. However, he seemed to not even notice Hawk.

But the strangest thing about Ian was the plump, white rat perched on his shoulder.

"Business or pleasure?" Ian asked Alex after giving her a hug.

"Business," she said.

"Is it urgent?"

She nodded.

"Come with me."

Hawk and Alex followed him around the corner to a small room with a pair of couches. The glass forming the outside walls were opaque enough to keep out any peeping Toms.

Ian gestured for them to both sit down and locked the door before taking a seat across from them. He held the back of his hand near his right shoulder and allowed his rat to walk off it. Hawk watched with wide-eyed amazement as Ian scooped up the rat and cuddled with it.

"What do you need help with?" Ian asked, dispensing with any formalities.

She placed the flash drive on the coffee table and slid the device to him. "It requires a RSA 4096 bit encryption key. Think you can crack it?"

Ian picked it up and studied the device. "How soon do you need it?"

"Tomorrow."

He drew back and shook his head. "No way. Do you know how difficult these things are to get into?"

"I do. Otherwise, I wouldn't be here. My skills have vastly improved since we last worked together."

"I'll see what I can do."

"Good," Alex said. "And I'll need to come with you."

Ian handed the device back to her. "That's a deal breaker for me. I'm not about to let you see where I live and work."

"Fine, but you better not let the device out of your sight."

"Agreed," Ian said. "Are you prepared to pay my fee?"

She nodded. "Is it still two hundred thousand Euros?"

"Two fifty now."

"Two fifty?"

"Inflation."

"I'll give you three hundred if you can get this back to me within twenty-four hours," Alex said.

"Fair enough," Ian said as he pocketed the drive. "I'll email you the wire instructions. Half of it up front."

"You'll have the money within the next fifteen minutes," she said as she stood. "I'm counting on you, Ian."

"Darling, have I ever let you down?"

Alex shook her head. "But let's not start now. This is by far the most important project I've ever been a part of."

"You know I'd do anything for you."

Ian replaced the rat to its previous position and then hugged Alex again. He offered a polite nod at Hawk, never once asking who he was or what he was doing here.

As they descended the steps, Hawk eased up next to Alex and spoke in her ear so she could hear over the music.

"That was weird," he said.

Alex was already on her phone, inputting the information required to wire fifty percent of Ian's fee.

"You didn't tell me the guy had a pet rat," Hawk said.

"There are some things that are best not to tell you about and simply let you experience them," she said.

"So, now what?"

"Now, we wait. And in the meantime, we dance."

Hawk sighed and followed Alex onto the floor, hoping that he could satiate her desire with no more than a song or two. But he knew that wasn't going to happen.

* * *

WHEN IAN RETURNED to his apartment, he dialed a number on his cell.

"What do you have for us?" the man on the other end asked.

"They showed up here, just like you predicted, Mr. Sinclair," Ian said.

"In that case, I'm sending you the file to pass along to them right now."

Ian smiled. "And the twenty million Euros?"

"I'll have my assistant wire you half now and the other half when you hand over the physical device. I'll have her text you the address for delivery."

"Excellent," Ian said before he hung up. He shoved the drive into his top drawer and closed it.

The night was still young.

CHAPTER 6

Charette Mesa
Mora, New Mexico

BLUNT HUNKERED DOWN on his seat, a converted five-gallon paint bucket, and poured piping hot coffee into the cap of his thermos. He watched the steam rise off the top before taking a sip.

"Ah," he said. "Now that'll put hair on your chest."

George Wickham, the deputy director of the Secret Service, chuckled. "If it put hair on my head, I might join you."

Blunt winked at him. "It obviously doesn't do that, does it?"

"Perhaps it's delivery method."

"Delivery method?"

"Yeah, J.D., technological innovations have come a long way since that thermos of yours was manufactured about fifty years ago."

Blunt grunted. "When I find something that works, I don't change."

"That's how you become a fossil," Wickham said.

Blunt shrugged as he drained the rest of his coffee. "You're only a fossil if you can't be effective. And I think based on our results we're pretty damn good at what we do."

"Is that why we're both reeling from the attack on the White House?"

"I'll admit that wasn't pretty," Blunt said. "But we tried to warn your boss. He wasn't having any of it. And he's the fossil now."

"Touché," Wickham said as he took Blunt's thermos lid and filled it with coffee. "So, what are we doing out here?"

"Isn't it obvious? We're trying to get a pronghorn, which at the moment feels about the same as trying to catch these terrorists infiltrating our country and government. They're everywhere."

"It's becoming far more difficult to tell friend from foe these days."

Blunt nodded. "Back in the day, we only had to look at someone to tell whose side they were on. But with the way Obsidian has infected our government, the enemy could be sitting right next to us and look just like we do."

Wickham scanned the plateau through his binoculars. "So, what are we gonna do about it?"

"We're gonna snuff them out, no matter how long

it takes. And we'll remind people what's made this country the greatest one in the world."

"And what's that?"

"Our undying devotion to freedom. We'll do anything to protect it for ourselves and help others preserve it. Freedom actually matters to us."

"As much as I want to believe this was about snagging a pronghorn, I think you really want to discuss some things."

Blunt nodded. "You've known me long enough to know that I'm not one to beat around the bush."

"Ain't that the truth. So, let's hear it. How are we gonna stop Obsidian from rotting our government to the core?"

"We're gonna deal with it the same way we handle Texas rattlesnakes," Blunt said. "You chop the head off."

"Do you know who's pulling the strings at Obsidian?"

Blunt picked up his binoculars and zeroed in on some movement on the horizon.

"See one?" Wickham asked.

"No, just a wild mustang kicking up dust," Blunt said, putting his binoculars down and directing his gaze at Wickham. "How familiar are you with Falcon Sinclair?"

"The Australian billionaire space entrepreneur?"

Blunt nodded.

"I don't know too much about him," Wickham said. "I just know he's trying to make space tourism a real thing. And from what I understand, he's giving Elon Musk a run for his money."

"He's also orchestrating a world takeover," Blunt said. "And I don't mean that in some metaphorical sense. Obsidian has agents all over the place or has compromised someone to do their bidding."

"Have they approached you?" Wickham asked.

"Not exactly, but they've tried to strong arm me into doing some things for them."

"And I trust you told them no."

Blunt kicked at the dirt. "Those bastards could offer me all the money in the world to give Falcon Sinclair a glass of water, and I wouldn't lift a finger."

"Well, I know there have been a few agents contacted, but they've reported the solicitation."

"That you know of," Blunt said.

"Sure, one or two of our agents could be on their payroll. But these guys are hard to reach without someone else knowing it. They do a good job of policing themselves."

"But you can't be positive, can you?"

"Not really. But we can monitor all their communiques outside of their work parameters. They know they're being spied on, which also dissuades that type of criminal behavior."

"Again though, you can't be positive that Obsidian doesn't have a couple of your guys feeding information back to Sinclair?"

"Well, no. But I know every single one of those men and—"

"Sinclair is trying to meet with the president," Blunt said, cutting off Wickham.

Wickham furrowed his brow. "Wait. What?"

"You heard me. Sinclair wants to meet with Young."

"What for?"

Blunt shrugged. "At this point, I'm not sure. But I can only guess that it's to entice him to do something that will benefit Obsidian."

"Well, that's news to me," Wickham said. "And every single off-site meeting must be vetted by our staff before it's approved. If Sinclair is trying to get a captive audience with Young, that's not going to happen unless we're able to sweep the area and do thorough background checks to make sure there's not a bad apple floating around the party meeting with the president. And you and I both know Sinclair would never agree to such stipulations."

"Sinclair would find a way around that somehow," Blunt said.

"Then I have to stop Young from meeting with him."

"That seems like the safest approach, but, again, we want to cut off the head of the snake, not just subdue it."

"What did you have in mind then?"

"Use Young to help us gather intel on Sinclair."

Wickham eyed Blunt closely. "You want the president to be a spy?"

Blunt nodded. "It's brilliant, isn't it?"

"No, it's lunacy. There's no telling what Sinclair would do to him if he found out, especially while they were meeting privately."

"Your men will be there with him, won't they?"

"One of them will be, per our standard protocol."

"Then let one of my agents go as a Secret Service agent and be the one in the room with Young. You know that my agents are more than capable of handling a situation like this."

Wickham sighed. "You know I can't do that, J.D."

"What's stopping you? Some ridiculous precedent? Throw that stuff out the window because we're all venturing into uncharted waters right now. If the president is meeting with a powerbroker, not for the interest of his own nation, but for his own selfish reasons, we're doomed. When will this end? This is our opportunity to do something about it."

"It's not that I don't trust your guys, but I can't do that."

"Come on, George. You know this is a golden chance to make headway in pulling the covers back on Obsidian. If you won't let Young spy, at least let one of my guys do it for you—and all while keeping Young safe."

"No, you come on, J.D. If you've got an agent preoccupied with gathering intel, his focus isn't going to be on the president. And protecting Young—that's the job. I think we'd be better off just convincing Young to reject any overtures from Sinclair."

"I'm afraid it might be too late for that," Blunt said.

"What are you not telling me?"

"Sinclair was at the First Lady's funeral and spoke with Young afterward."

"And you were privy to their conversation?" Wickham asked.

"No, but—"

"Then don't worry about it. I'll do my best to make sure Young doesn't set foot anywhere near Sinclair."

"I think that'd be a mistake," Blunt said.

"Look, you focus on your job, and it'll all be fine. You go get the head of that snake on your own. Your people are more than capable of doing that."

Blunt sighed and nodded, resigning himself to the fact that he couldn't make a compelling enough case for Wickham.

Blunt tapped Wickham on the shoulder and pointed to a nearby ridge. "There's your pronghorn."

Wickham dropped to his knees and took his time putting the pronghorn in the middle of his crosshairs. Blunt trained his binoculars on the lone animal meandering around the edge of the cliff and cut his gaze over at Wickham.

Just as he pulled the trigger, Wickham flinched, resulting in a missed shot.

"Well, damn," Wickham said. "I thought I had him."

Blunt nodded knowingly. "I know. I thought so too."

CHAPTER 7

Washington, D.C.

WHEN THE PHOENIX FOUNDATION team returned to headquarters two days later, Blunt was anxiously awaiting some good news. Blunt was also concerned that President Young would be pressuring the intelligence community for a quick win against terrorists as opposed to focusing on Obsidian's plot. Both targets needed to be handled, but Obsidian was the far more urgent of the two.

A half-hour into Blunt's work day, he found out just how desperate the president was. Blunt took a call and was greeted by Young's secretary.

"Please hold for the President," she said.

That announcement used to excite Blunt, but now he was dreading it. He never enjoyed telling the president what he didn't want to hear.

"Good morning, J.D.," Young said when he finally connected on the line.

"Mr. President, it's good to hear your voice again," Blunt said.

"You too," Young said. "I was getting tired of talking to nurses and doctors and morticians."

"That was a lovely service for Madeline. You let me know if there's anything I can do for you."

"How about tracking down Evana Bahar?"

"Evana's organization wasn't the one responsible for the bombing."

"You don't know that."

"It's highly unlikely that they would've been able to orchestrate such an inside attack. On the other hand, Obsidian is—"

"I don't care about Obsidian," Young bellowed. "They're some shadow organization that nobody knows much about. We're not sure they really exist. But Evana Bahar *is* real, and if we don't track her down soon, she may soon lead Al Fatihin to strike again."

"We'll do our best," Blunt said.

"Do better. Make her a top priority. I'll be in touch for progress reports."

Young hung up, leaving Blunt frustrated. His angst only continued to grow when he met with Hawk and Alex in the conference room an hour later.

Blunt found his two agents sitting around the table and sifting through intelligence reports. After lumbering to his seat at the head of the table, he dumped out a stack of folders.

"Please tell me that you got some actionable intel off that flash drive," Blunt said.

Alex shook her head as she slid some documents toward him. "I'm not sure if Timmons had been holed up on that island for so long that he just had to get out, but there wasn't anything of consequence on that device."

"Nothing?"

"It looked like a few stolen weapons plans from Colton Industries, but nothing to write home about," Alex said.

"So we're back to square one?" he asked.

"As far as knowing what Obsidian is up to, yes," Hawk said. "We're still in the dark as far as how they intend to accomplish their end game."

"At least we know what their aim is: world power," Blunt said. "But we still need to know the *how* if we intend to stop them."

"And the president? How is he?" Alex asked.

"Fully recovered and ornery as ever," Blunt said. "Which means that he's back to becoming a pain in our ass if we don't track down Evana Bahar."

Hawk shook his head. "We haven't any reports about her in a while, so it's safe to assume she's gone underground. We can't exactly manufacture something if she's gone into hiding."

"I think we need to stay on Obsidian," Alex said. "Despite this latest setback with Timmons, we're getting closer to unmasking what this organization doing. We need to keep the pressure on."

"Easy for you to say since you don't have to juggle the politics," Blunt said.

A faint smile spread across Alex's lips. "That's why you get paid the big bucks."

"See what else you can learn about Falcon Sinclair, and we'll talk later today," Blunt said before dismissing the meeting.

He returned to his office with a note that CIA Deputy Director Randy Wood had left a message. Blunt sat down and dialed Wood's number.

"What do you need?" Blunt asked Wood when he answered.

"I got some information that might interest you and your team," Wood said.

"Fire away," Blunt said. "I could use some good news."

"We just got a hit about an hour ago on a device we've been tracking that belongs to Madeline Young."

"You found her?" Blunt asked. "Isn't this going to present a problem since we just buried her?"

"Sure it will, which is why I'm turning this over to you," Wood said.

"Where is she?"

"Cape Verde, relaxing beachside from what I understand at a private resort there. I'm sure she might be willing to talk once you ply her with booze."

"You really do want me to get in hot water with Young, don't you?"

"If you're that concerned about staying in his good graces, there's always Andrei Orlovsky you can use," Wood said.

Blunt's eyebrows shot upward. "You have Orlovsky?"

"Caught him last night in a sting we set up in Algeria. Nobody knows about it, so you could have him set up some kind of weapons sale with Evana Bahar. That ought to draw her out of hiding."

"Let me mull this over and discuss it with my team," Blunt said. "You're giving me two can't lose situations at once."

"I aim to please," Wood said. "Just don't hurt Madeline. She might prove to be helpful in the future."

"You have far more faith in her than I do," Blunt said.

"I simply know her, that's all. She'll do anything to save her own bacon, even if that means returning to the U.S. and groveling at the president's feet. In any case, I'm sure you'll be surprised by how much she offers up."

Blunt called Hawk and Alex back to his office and briefed them on the developing situation.

"So, which one do you two want to pursue first?" Blunt asked.

Alex cocked her head to one side and furrowed her brow. "Is there even a question about this?"

"I agree," Hawk said. "It's got to be Madeline Young. We need all the intel we can get on Obsidian."

"Then off you go," Blunt said. "I'll have to figure out a way to appease Young in the meantime."

"That's what you do best," Hawk said.

CHAPTER 8

Santa Maria, Cape Verde

HAWK TUGGED ON HIS cap and looked at Alex. She smiled as she tucked a tuft of his dark locks flaring out of the side of his hat. After looking him up and down, she patted his bare chest and gave him a playful push.

"You know I don't feel right about this," he said while adjusting his pants.

"What? Using your body to get information?"

He nodded. "I have a policy against that, something my wife might understand."

"You're just using those rock hard abs of yours and sculpted chest to get Madeline Young's attention, that's all," she said before patting him on his rear end.

"I feel like a piece of meat right now."

"You'll feel much better when you get the chance to interrogate her so we can stop Obsidian."

"I'd rather wear a dress," Hawk said. "That would at least be a disguise."

Alex giggled. "Just pretend like this is a Bollywood movie and flaunt it since you've got it."

Hawk grunted. "If you would've told me that my life as a black ops asset would include playing the role of cabana boy, I would've never signed up."

"Just get out there already," Alex said before pulling his arm and then ushering him to the door.

Hawk surveyed the area, noticing not much more than a pool and scantily clad people in and around it. Madeline was lounging near the Sol Hotel Resort pool, sipping a piña colada. The glass was almost empty, and she studied it while chewing on her lip.

"Would you look at that?" Hawk said on his coms. "This is just disgusting. She's trying to entice some man into buying her another drink."

"And that man is going to be you," Alex said. "Enough already and buy her a drink."

Hawk cozied up to the bar and ordered a piña colada for the First Lady. While he would've preferred to walk up to her and have a conversation, he noticed a pair of guards tucked away in the shadows. He identified three and asked Alex to keep an eye out for them.

"I see them," she said. "As if they don't stand out here like a sore thumb. Everybody's in bikinis and board shorts except for the hotel staff and her security detail."

"Are you ready?" Hawk asked.

"Born ready," Alex said.

"All right. Here it goes."

He snagged a stray glass on a stand next to one of the lounge chairs and waited for his drink. After the waiter handed it to Hawk, he meandered around the pool and eased into the seat next to Madeline. She wore a white bikini with a see-through shawl. Her pink sunhat was pulled down just above the top of her sunglasses. If Hawk didn't already know she was here, he never would've spotted her reclining in her chair like a common tourist.

She appeared to be halfway through the latest Jodi Picoult novel and didn't exhibit any signs of nervousness, blissfully unaware that the past she was running from was about to confront her head on.

Hawk had selected an appropriate suitor while waiting at the bar, a distinguished looking man who had announced he was about to finish his drink and then leave. All Hawk had left to do was deliver the message.

"*Senhora?*" Hawk said.

"Yes," she said, placing her book face down and then turning toward Hawk.

"*Senhora*, that man over at the bar in the white suit asked me to deliver this drink to you," he said.

She looked him up and down. "I'd rather it be from you."

"Sorry to disappoint you, *senhora*. I'm not allowed to interact with resort patrons on that level."

"What exactly did you think I was suggesting?"

Hawk left the tray by Madeline's table and walked off.

"Is she talking the bait?" he asked over his coms.

"She just stood and is navigating toward the bar," Alex said.

"Phase two," he said. "Are you ready?"

Seconds later, Madeline glided past the bar and headed straight toward the men's restroom. One of her security team members left the shadows and started following her. She turned around and cast a leery eye toward him. Receiving the unspoken message, he spun around and returned to his post.

Hawk shot furtive glances at Madeline as she approached the door. She poked her head inside and looked around before slipping into the restroom.

* * *

EVEN BEFORE THE PHOENIX Foundation learned the truth behind the attack on the White House, Alex wasn't the biggest Madeline Young fan. Alex found the First Lady's humanitarian work little more than photo ops for the press to show what a compassionate woman she was. Behind the scenes, the

Secret Service agents who worked Madeline's details described her as monstrous and narcissistic, her elite roots shining through and standing in stark contrast to the president's rural upbringing and authentic behavior. Madeline Young once sold the evening gown she wore to the Oscars with the caveat that it must be sold for more than she bought it for. She demanded the bidding start at two hundred thousand. From that moment on, Alex dreamed of connecting on one solid punch to Madeline Young's face.

Alex's big opportunity had arrived.

With the men's bathroom completely empty, Alex took up a position in the stall at the far end. She placed a pair of Hawk's shoes on the ground to give the impression that there was indeed a man behind the door.

The clicking of heels alerted Alex to the fact that the First Lady had finally arrived. Her reputation as a philanderer proved to be a simple target. Alex could only assume it was the thousands of miles of ocean between Madeline and the U.S. that lured her into a sense of false security. Or maybe she lacked self-control or was confident that Falcon Sinclair would soon control the world and help her navigate a way back to the public eye in a redemption story that would inspire a new generation. The reasoning was of no consequence as Madeline Young wasn't taking any precautions to protect her identity on foreign soil.

Alex listened as Madeline approached the final stall.

"Boo, are you in here?" Madeline asked.

An amused Hawk who was standing just outside the door chuckled over the coms.

I wonder if that means Hawk wants me to call him Boo.

Madeline finally arrived in front of Alex's stall. "There you are. The least you could do would be to give me a signal of some sort. Now, what do you say we go somewhere really private and—"

Madeline stopped mid-sentence and froze. Despite her strains, Alex couldn't even hear the First Lady breathing.

After a pregnant pause, the door flew open and was followed by Madeline Young. As she realized that her Boo was another woman, the First Lady went slack-jawed. Alex seized her chance, leaping off the toilet and lunging toward Madeline. She put her hands up to protect herself from the onslaught of oncoming fury. The idea was to absorb the first few blows and then strike back.

But instead of fighting, Madeline spun around and raced to safety. But Alex didn't fly several thousand miles to return home without a single answer, much less get outwitted by a woman she'd grown to loathe. Alex scrambled across the wet tile floor and dove at Madeline's feet. Grabbing just enough of her heels,

Alex tripped up the First Lady and sent her flying backward into the bank of sinks. She finally came to rest against the brick wall, her head slamming hard into it. Madeline moaned as she tried to get up.

"Keep it down," Alex said, her gun trained in front of her as she walked over to Madeline. "I'd suggest not giving me any reason to shoot you either."

"What do you want?" Madeline asked, placing her hands in the air.

"I want you to tell me about Falcon Sinclair," Alex said as she brandished her weapon.

"Put the gun away. I'll tell you what you want to know. There's no need to get violent."

Alex didn't flinch. "Talk."

"Okay, fine. He's rich beyond your wildest dreams, though not quite as charming as he fancies himself to—"

Alex narrowed her eyes. "Tell me something I can't know by reading the supermarket tabloids."

"I'm not sure what you're after, so I'm afraid you're going to need to be a bit more specific."

"What is he planning?"

The First Lady shrugged. "Beats me. All I know is that he told me to come here and eventually he'd return me to the public eye."

"Did he give you any indication of when that might be?"

"He called me last night and said within the next week he'd have a better idea of when that would happen."

Alex jammed her gun into Madeline's temple. "What is he planning?"

"I swear I don't know. General Fortner told me Sinclair was working on some weapon, but I never learned anything else about it, though that wasn't for a lack of trying."

"Fortner didn't trust you," Alex said as she backed off.

"Yeah, and look where that got him. If you think you're going to get me to cry about that, forget about it. Fortner was a means to an end for me. I needed to get out of the White House. The demands were suffocating. And Noah wasn't about to let me live elsewhere because of how it would hurt his image."

"I don't believe this was just about a floundering marriage. What did Sinclair promise you?"

"Peace and prosperity, the usual."

Alex glared at Madeline. "You're lying."

"Look, if you're going to shoot me, get it over with. Otherwise, I'm leaving. I've told you everything I know."

Madeline stood and tried to push her way past Alex. But she rammed the barrel of her weapon into Madeline's chest.

"We're not finished," Alex said. "I could shoot you and nobody would ever know. You're not leaving until I'm satisfied."

Madeline held her ground. "You might shoot me, but you'll never get away with it. I've told you everything I know, but if you insist on keeping me here, all I have to do is scream for my guards to rush in and kill you right here with no questions asked. So unless you're into mutually assured destruction, I'd advise you to step aside and look elsewhere for your answers."

"Let her go, Alex," Hawk said over the coms. "We don't need this to turn into a mess."

Alex slid over, enabling Madeline to pass.

Once the First Lady disappeared around the corner, Alex holstered her weapon, tucking it in the back of her pants and out of sight.

"It's clear," Hawk said. "Let's get out of here before Madeline gets any other ideas. We have what we need."

"And what's that?" she asked.

"Falcon Sinclair is developing a weapon."

"We've known that for a while."

"We've only assumed he was building something. Now we know. And we also know he's planning on using it very soon."

"That's just a hunch," she said.

"No," Hawk said. "Falcon Sinclair isn't the kind of man to patiently wait. The minute his weapon is operational, he's going to use it. And if he's going to have more information within the next week about when Madeline Young can return to life as normal, that means something is about to go down."

"But what exactly?" Alex asked.

"That's what we need to find out—and fast."

CHAPTER 9

Washington, D.C.

BLUNT EYED THE BOTTLE of bourbon in the bottom of his desk and checked his watch. He deliberated whether it was too early to get into it. Despite the fact that it was 11:00 a.m., he felt tempted to imbibe. Anything to take the edge off from the pressure building from within and outside in the form of President Young.

Blunt chose to stay dry for a few more hours as his two agents were due to return at any moment with a more in-depth report about what happened in Cape Verde. The shortened version he'd already received painted a bleak picture, one where the First Lady knew the obvious but nothing beyond that. But the intelligence community needed more to act on if the government planned to be proactive to the events occurring both in the open and in the shadows. A half-hour passed, and he decided that he couldn't wait any longer. He dumped a healthy portion of bourbon into his thermos and lumbered to the conference room. While waiting for Hawk and Alex, Blunt took a seat at the table directly across from the television and propped his feet up on the desk. He took a long pull before smacking his lips and screwing the top back onto the bottle.

After turning on the television, he surfed through several channels before coming to rest—against his better judgment—on a cable news program where a panel of various Washington insiders were discussing the news of the day. Blunt hated shows like this one, but the question on the screen caught his eye.

"This is what we're talking about today," announced Herb Kingman as he gestured toward the bank of screens behind him. "A Rasmussen poll released this morning showed that seventy percent of Americans don't feel safe. Seventy percent. That's an astounding number for this country, especially considering that the highest level since the 9/11 attacks was right around forty percent."

"That's right, Herb," chimed in Samantha Hunt. "This is the first poll that's been conducted since the White House was struck with a bomb, which makes some of the details even more eye-opening. Since terrorists first assaulted us on our own soil, fears about future attacks have been largely weighted along partisan lines. When a Democrat was in office, Republicans were more fearful and vice-versa. But under Noah Young, political affiliation made no discernible difference in how people felt."

"This just goes to show you that people feel very unsettled right now," Herb said. "And we still haven't even received confirmation about who was behind this. Up until this point, Al Fatihin has been the terrorist organization that Americans have feared the most, but since they remained oddly silent about this latest event other than to celebrate it, we're left to wonder if there's another terrorist cell on the rise that we should be concerned with."

"Yes, and we want to dive further into that topic with former Homeland Security Deputy Gene Pinkston," Samantha said as she turned toward the longtime bureaucrat.

What a disaster! Pinkston couldn't stop a four year old with a water pistol.

When Pinkston's face appeared on the screen, Blunt had enough and turned off the television. He and Pinkston had gone round and round on policy, which Blunt felt was often detrimental to the country's safety. Nevertheless, the two remained friends. But Blunt wasn't about to waste his time listening to Pinkston's fear mongering.

Blunt returned to the reports in front of him while

waiting for Hawk and Alex to arrive. After fifteen minutes, Blunt's phone rang with a call from CIA Deputy Director Randy Wood.

"Have you put together an op to track down Madeline Young?" Wood asked after the two exchanged pleasantries.

"I've got two agents about to walk into headquarters here any moment now and give me a full report," Blunt said.

"And the abbreviated version?"

"Nothing that we didn't already know," Blunt said.

"That's just as well because we've got something else that needs more immediate attention."

Blunt chuckled. "The tyranny of the urgent. Isn't that how it always is?"

"It's no joke this time," Wood said. "I know we get this a lot, but I was just in on a scathing call from the president, who's up in arms about this new poll about how unsafe Americans feel. Have you seen that yet?"

"I just saw it. The merchants of fear are doing a great job of stirring up the people this time."

"I agree," Wood said. "But that doesn't change the fact that the people who really do the grunt work to keep Americans safe from outside threats are going to be summarily fired if the president carries through with some of his threats."

Blunt stood and paced around the room. "I just

spoke with him a couple of days ago and told him that I'd try to track down Evana Bahar, but she seems to have gone underground. I know Young is concerned with the optics of that attack on the White House and doesn't want his poll numbers to take a nose dive as the next election cycle is getting ready to gear up, but there's only so much we can do. The last report I read about her said that Al Fatihin was struggling to raise capital for more weapons. If she can't fight, she's not going to come out of hiding."

"Agreed. But I'm afraid that's not going to quell the president's concerns. He said he wants to be able to address the American people to allay their fears and soon. And he wants to do it with the capture of someone prominent."

"In that case, I need Orlovsky," Blunt said.

"Define the word *need*," Wood said.

"We need him physically in our possession to lure Bahar into the open."

"Not gonna happen."

"Won't or can't?" Blunt asked.

"The president has been clear that Orlovsky is to remain in custody, utilized as an asset for information only."

"What is the purpose of that?"

"From what I understand, he doesn't want to risk losing him, much less anyone else finding out that he's been apprehended. It works to our advantage that nobody knows he's been compromised."

Blunt sighed. "I get that, but if Young won't let us utilize the best chance we have at drawing out Bahar, he's tying our hands. He might as well parade Orlovsky on camera so he has something to thump his chest about."

"Look, I hate the political side of this as much as you do."

"It's why I left the senate," Blunt said. "I wanted to get away from this bureaucratic shit storm that always rolled downhill on me. And now it's happening again, only it's hurting our country's security this time."

"Unfortunately, we can't get away from that."

Blunt grunted and said nothing.

"What are you thinking, J.D.?"

"I need to at least speak with Orlovsky so I can set something up."

"Talking with him is the only thing you can do."

"I'm going to need to incentivize him, too," Blunt said. "Give me the power to authorize something that would make his life more comfortable."

"I'll see what I can do," Wood said. "Just know that I'll work as hard as I can to get you what you need. I just can't *give* you Orlovsky."

"I understand. We'll adjust accordingly. But for the record, I don't like it."

"I'll be in touch."

Blunt hung up and sat back down. He pushed Wood to see if he could set up the ideal situation with Orlovsky, but the roadblock wasn't the end of the world. The situation would present more of a challenge without a doubt. However, Blunt was confident he could utilize a compliant Orlovsky.

A few minutes later, Hawk and Alex walked through the door and greeted Blunt. He glanced at his watch.

"You're late," Blunt said.

"It was a long trip back," Hawk said. "But you're not usually so concerned with how prompt we are. What's eating at you?"

"The president is threatening to pull the plug on the Phoenix Foundation if we don't get him a win," Blunt said.

"A win?" Alex asked. "We could reveal that his wife is a traitor."

"That's not the kind of thing he's looking for," Blunt said. "He needs something that's going to turn the poll numbers around."

"What do you need us to do?" Hawk asked.

"As much as it pains me to say this, we're going to need to table our pursuit of Obsidian for the time being," Blunt said.

"You've got to be joking," Alex said. "We just flew

to Cape Verde and—"

"I don't like it any more than you do," Blunt said. "But with the pressure Young is putting on us, we can't just ignore his demands. Sometimes we must play the political game."

"Politics," Hawk said. "It's ruining this country."

"I won't disagree with you," Blunt said, "but it's a necessary evil at the moment. We want everyone in this country to feel safe at night when they lay their head on a pillow to go to sleep."

"So, what now?" Hawk asked.

"I'm going to have Andrei Orlovsky arrange a meeting for us with Evana Bahar," Blunt said.

"You think he's going to help us?" Alex asked.

"We'll do our best to make him want to help us," Blunt said. "But you leave that to me. Just go home and get ready for a flight to Afghanistan. We're going to flush her out."

"Sounds like my kind of plan," Hawk said.

"Good," Blunt said. "I'm counting on you to deliver for us. I'll call you later with the details."

Hawk and Alex exited the room, leaving Blunt to ponder his next move. He needed to make a good one. Not only did the fate of The Phoenix Foundation depend upon his ability to craft a plausible scenario, but so did the safety of the country.

Blunt needed another drink.

CHAPTER 10

BLUNT NEEDED TO RELAX. Each looming decision weighed heavily on him as he considered the best path forward. Preventing Obsidian from getting its tentacles into President Young appeared to be the highest priority. And if funding for the black ops program was lost, Blunt would be powerless to do anything in the future. However, he was willing to sacrifice all of it to save his niece, Morgan. He couldn't live with himself if she became an innocent casualty in this shadow war.

Based on the information he'd gathered about how Obsidian operated, Blunt was concerned about Morgan's treatment. He could only imagine how scared she was, especially since she probably never considered that she could be a pawn in a terrorist's game before officially becoming part of the intelligence community. Blunt needed to get her out of there as soon as possible since rescuing her meant he could warn Young about how dangerous Falcon Sinclair really was.

With Hawk and Alex set to travel to Afghanistan, Blunt only had one other option to help with his niece: Titus Black.

Blunt called his other operative and briefed him on the mission.

"Are you sure this is something you want to do?" Black asked. "If something goes wrong, this situation won't end well for her."

"Do you think you're going to fail?"

"Of course not," Black said. "But that's before I know exactly what this rescue will entail. You've told me the end game—"

"Something you aren't to tell anyone else about," Blunt said.

"That goes without saying, sir. You've told me what you want, but I still have no operational details, starting with the location of the facility and the blueprints for it."

"I'll have that for you in the morning. I've got someone working on it for me. Triangulating their exact location has been quite challenging since they're routing their calls all over the place. They are professionals in every sense of the word, but I'm confident that we'll be able to pinpoint where they are."

"None of this seems ideal for an op of this magnitude," Black said. "Knowing that this is your niece I'm attempting to save should make you more cautious, not less."

"What choice do I have?" Blunt said, his voice quivering. "I can't let them do this to her."

"How did they even find out about her?" Black asked. "I didn't even know you had a niece."

"It's not something I advertise, but I do have a half-sister. We were never really close, but her daughter reached out to me recently after she learned who I was. Our relationship has mostly consisted of writing letters back and forth, but I never would've considered anyone would target her."

"Obsidian seems to know everything about everyone."

"Which makes the idea of that group taking over sectors of world governments even more terrifying," Blunt said.

"After what I've learned about how they function, that's a rational fear. Whatever you need me to do, just let me know. I'll do whatever it takes to get her back safely."

Blunt thanked Black and ended the call. If there was one thing the Phoenix Foundation director needed, it was to strip off the shackles that Obsidian had placed on him. And that wasn't going to happen until Morgan was home safely.

A half-hour later, Blunt's phone buzzed.

"Please tell me you have some good news," he said as he answered.

Mallory Kauffman sighed. "You're always about business these days."

"You should know as well as anyone that you never know who's listening in on your conversation," Blunt said.

"Of course, but perhaps you're forgetting that I know how to get recorded conversations erased, too."

"There are some things that are always best said in person," Blunt said.

She chuckled. "Well, all you have to do is invite me over."

Blunt smiled. He was surprised when he first learned Mallory's interest in him extended beyond his professional life. And before she started giving off signals that she was interested in him, he couldn't remember the last time that his heart even fluttered for a second over a woman. Given the fact that Mallory was a quarter of a century his junior, he never once considered her in a romantic sense despite the fact that he found her attractive. He thought that chapter of his life was closed after his wife died. But Mallory had rekindled something in him he thought had burned out long ago. He would've preferred to devote his spare time to their burgeoning relationship, but the timing wasn't ideal.

"Soon," Blunt said. "I promise."

"Have you told your team?" she asked.

"Told them what?"

"Oh, come on, J.D. You know what I'm talking about. Have you told them about us?"

"I'm not sure what to tell them, but I don't know when I'd do it. We're all so busy right now figuring out a way to stop Obsidian from compromising every branch of our government."

"Well, I guess you can add me to that list of people working tirelessly for you," she said. "Tracking down this location for you wasn't easy."

"Please tell me you figured it out," he said.

"I did. I'm going to text you the coordinates of the location. Now, would you mind telling me exactly what was so important about this call?"

"I wish I could but—"

"J.D.! If I'm sticking my neck out for you, the least you can do is let me know why."

Blunt sighed. "You can't tell anyone, but Obsidian has my niece."

"They what?"

"Yeah, and they're going to hold her hostage until Falcon Sinclair has had a chance to meet with President Young. That's why this is so important."

"Why didn't you tell me sooner?"

"I don't want anyone questioning my motives right now or thinking that I've been compromised."

"But you have and—"

"I'm handling it," he said. "Once I get my niece back, I'll be able to steer this situation in a more favorable direction. In the meantime, I need to keep walking this tightrope that has my stomach in knots."

"Okay, well if you need me to do anything else for you to help, just let me know. You can't let this drag on much longer. There's much more at stake here."

"I know," Blunt said. "But what would you do? Would you sacrifice an innocent family member? Sometimes, we have to make hard choices, but that's not what I'm willing to make at the moment. She doesn't deserve this."

"And neither do the American people."

"Of course not, but I have no intention of letting it get that far. And thanks to you, I don't think I'll have to. Just keep this bit of information to yourself, okay?"

"Be careful, J.D. I don't like this."

"Me either. And it'll be behind me soon enough. Now, I have to go, but thanks for getting the location for me. You have no idea how truly grateful I am."

"I'll be in touch," she said. "We need to get together soon, and not so we can talk about work, if you know what I mean."

Blunt smiled. "I know exactly what you mean. And we will soon enough."

He hung up and sank back into his chair.

I'm coming for you, Falcon Sinclair.

CHAPTER 11

HAWK CHECKED HIS WATCH as he paced around the hangar outside the airplane. The pilot flying Hawk and Alex to Afghanistan still hadn't shown up and was now fifteen minutes late.

"Should we call Blunt and find out what's going on?" Alex asked.

"Let's give Captain Covington five more minutes before we make that call," Hawk said. "I'm not interested in waking Blunt up at this time of night."

Hawk cupped his hands together and blew on them in an effort to take the bite out of the early morning chill hanging in the air. If the pilot never showed up, Hawk figured it would be for the best, preferring to continue the Phoenix Foundation's pursuit of Obsidian, namely Falcon Sinclair.

But with a president who was not only embarrassed over the gross breach of security but also grieving over the loss of his wife, Hawk didn't anticipate Young having a change of heart anytime soon. The truth about Madeline, however, had the potential to change everything, though Blunt believed such news would make Young more red-faced and all but guaranteed a single term. After everything the team endured under Young's predecessor, Hawk understood the reasoning. He just wasn't sure he agreed with it.

In the distance, a pair of headlights flickered as a car roared toward them.

"Looks like Kip finally decided to show up," Alex said.

"Go easy on him," Hawk said. "He's never been late before. I'm sure there's a good reason for it."

"I hope you're right."

"Before you go nuclear on him, just remember how he saved us in the Cocos Islands."

"Fine," Alex huffed. "I'm just ready to get in the air and finish planning this op."

Hawk turned his attention back toward the vehicle racing toward them. The sun still hung below the horizon, but dawn was clearly breaking. They were supposed to already be in the air, but the co-pilot for the long trip had started running through the checklist to ensure as prompt of a takeoff as possible.

Kip Covington had always been a great friend to the Phoenix Foundation team, maintaining discretion about their meetings and never asking any questions.

Hawk figured if Kip ever wanted to write a behind-the-scenes book about the adventures of flying around secret agents, most people would dismiss the stories as pure fiction. Kip had experienced plenty while flying Hawk and Alex around, and just having him at the helm made Hawk feel more confident about the mission.

Kip parked his car near the gate and then trudged toward the plane, his face pale.

"Everything all right?" Hawk asked. "You don't look so good."

"Morning, Hawk," Kip said in a raspy voice before breaking into a cough. "I've had this nasty cold I can't seem to shake."

"Should you be flying today?" Alex asked.

"I'll be fine. I just need to get some coffee in me and I'll be fine."

"Roger that," Hawk said.

"I brought some water bottles for the trip," Kip said. "Do you two want some?"

"Sure," Alex said as she grabbed a couple and then handed one to Hawk.

Hawk and Alex boarded the plane while Kip completed their pre-flight checklist. Fifteen minutes later, they were airborne. For the next two hours, Hawk and Alex went over all the details from their plan to capture Evana Bahar. Blunt leveraged more comfortable cell conditions for Orlovsky to get him to comply with a request to arrange a meeting to discuss discounted weapons with the Al Fatihin leader.

"Do you think Evana is going to show up?" Alex asked.

"Orlovsky requested her specifically in the email he sent to her secret account," Hawk said. "Based on the intel we have about her trying to scrounge up enough funds to buy some more weapons, I'd be shocked if she didn't show."

"Getting her there is ninety percent of this op."

"That's why I'm confident this mission is going to be a success," Hawk said. "At least we'll be able to get the pressure off Blunt and get back to focusing on Obsidian."

"I hope you're right," she said. "I'm going to catch some more shuteye. We've got a big day ahead of us."

"I'm with you on that," Hawk said as he reclined his seat and fell asleep.

* * *

THE PILOT POSING as Kip Covington checked his flight path to make sure that they were squarely over Russian territory. Crashing the plane there would keep the incident off the international radar. Earlier that evening, Len Bukov had murdered the real Kip

Covington and covered his body in weights, sinking him to the bottom of the Potomac. By the time anyone discovered Kip's remains—if ever—the U.S. government would've likely forgotten all about the pilot for the clandestine operation.

The co-pilot remained slumped over, out cold from the syringe laced with a drug Bukov had injected into the man's neck an hour into the flight. Easing open the cockpit door, Bukov peeked out to see if drugs had taken effect on the other passengers. He smiled as he noticed both Hawk and Alex reclining in their seats, eyes closed.

"Dead asleep," Bukov whispered to himself. "An appropriate description."

He would've preferred to shoot them both or, at the very least, remove all the parachutes. But his instructions were to crash the plane in Russia. When the bodies were returned to the U.S., Russia wanted to make sure that there was no appearance of foul play.

Bukov returned to his seat and issued a May Day call over the radio. After hearing a response from a nearby tower, he left the cockpit and locked the door. Then he strapped on a parachute. Next he ripped off the mask that enabled him to pass as Kip Covington and disengaged the voice simulator fastened to his chest.

"Sweet dreams," Bukov said before opening the plane door and plunging into darkness.

CHAPTER 12

Miami, Florida

TITUS BLACK CROUCHED LOW as he moved along the side of the aluminum storage facility near the docks. Black craned his neck around the corner to see if anyone was near the entrance. A pelican lit on one of the pylons nearby and squawked. Seconds later, a guard poked his head out of the door and scanned the area before returning inside.

"I hate those damn birds," J.D. Blunt said over the coms. He and Christina Shields, who provided Black with support for most of their missions, were situated in the Phoenix Foundation offices watching the scene from Black's body cam.

"That makes two of us," Black said.

"Three," chimed in Shields.

Blunt's contact at the CIA had traced the last proof-of-life call back to this warehouse in Miami, which was owned by a shell corporation operating out of the Bahamas. A few dollars to entice the right people resulted in the name of the person who actually registered the business, a known associate of Falcon Sinclair.

"How many hostiles am I dealing with?" Black asked.

"I see three heat signatures," Shields said.

"So, two and the package?"

"Roger that," she said.

"Her name's Morgan," Blunt said with a growl. "She's not just some random person you're extracting."

"No need to get in a huff," Black said. "I treat every one of these people as if they were my own kin. It's just a quicker way of communicating."

Blunt grunted loud enough for Black to hear it in his earpiece. That sound was familiar, a signal that Blunt was either bemused or moving on. Either way, the topic was closed.

"You shouldn't meet any resistance until you turn the corner of the long corridor just behind the receptionist desk," Shields said.

"Copy," Black said as he approached the front door. He placed his hand on it and tugged.

"It's locked," he said. "Wanna give me a hand here, Shields?"

"One second," she said, the furious clicking of a keyboard clattering in the background. "Almost there."

The door came ajar, and Black grabbed the handle.

"Your voodoo with these security systems never ceases to amaze me," he said in a hushed tone.

He pulled open the glass door and eased inside.

"All the hostiles are congregated in a room near the back on the right side of the hallway," Shields said. "They've been making the rounds every fifteen minutes or so but just finished the latest one."

"Roger that," Black said as he crept past the front desk.

The loud voice of a man from the other side of the room startled Black as a monitor in the waiting area flickered to life.

"Welcome to TenTrack Industries," the man said, "where the future is today."

Black sighed in relief as he sank down with his back against the front desk.

"What the hell is that?" Blunt asked.

"It looks like some kind of welcome video," Shields said.

Then she let out a slew of expletives.

"What is it?" Black asked.

"You're about to have company," Shields said.

Black scrambled behind the desk as he heard footfalls approaching his location.

"I thought we turned that damn thing off," one of the guards groused.

"Me too," the other man said. "Maybe you just moved the switch to motion control activation instead of—"

The conversation ended abruptly before the doors creaked opened.

"Be careful," Shield said over the coms. "You've got two hostiles."

Black smiled at his good fortune. Both guards in the same room as him and unaware of his presence.

Like shooting fish in a barrel.

Black rose and fired at the two men. He hit the first one in the head and the second guy in the neck. They both collapsed. Black put another round in each of them to ensure the job was completed before heading toward the back.

"We've got a problem," Shields said.

"I don't like the sound of that," Black said.

"The third heat signature just left the building."

"What are you trying to say?" he asked.

"It's not the package," Shields said.

"How many times do I have to tell you that her name is Morgan?" Blunt said with a growl.

Black raced toward the back and hit the door only to find it locked.

"Uh, Shields, I need a way out of here," he said.

"What's wrong?" she asked.

Black stared at the contraption in the middle of

the room with enough explosives to annihilate a small town.

"There's a bomb in here, set to blow in one minute," he explained.

"What's the situation with the doors?" she asked.

"They all have a key pad along with a retinal scanner."

"The retinal part is easy now," she said.

"I need the other part thirty seconds ago," Black said as he sprinted to the lobby.

He dragged one guard's body over to the front door near the security panel.

"Still accessing," she said.

"Please hurry. I've got thirty-five seconds remaining by my count."

"Almost there," she said. "Got it."

She rattled off a long series of digits that she found on the TenTrack Industries mainframe, numbers designed to act as a master code. Once he finished that, a yellow light started blinking on the pad just below the scanner. Black hoisted up the guard's body so his head was even with the device and then peeled back his eyelids. The machine on the wall whirred and beeped.

"Come on," Black said.

A click released the lock and Black wasted no time, dropping the body and sprinting outside. He was only about twenty feet clear of the building before an explosion rocked the ground. The blast sent Black diving to avoid the heat and shrapnel that flew out of the front doors.

Black rolled to a stop and took cover behind a nearby truck. He glanced around the side of the building and saw a car racing out of the parking lot. Black took a few shots at the driver but didn't hit him.

"Want the good news first or the bad news?" Black asked.

"If you don't have Morgan, nothing you're going to say is good news," Blunt said over the coms.

"In that case, I'll just spell it out for you," Black said. "One of the guards got away, but Morgan is obviously still alive."

"Like I said," Black growled, "if you don't have Morgan, there's no good news. But at least you used her name this time."

Black exhaled before hustling to his feet. Sirens wailed in the distance. He didn't want to be around in five minutes when the place was crawling with local law enforcement officials.

***

BLUNT LOOKED AT SHIELDS before slamming his fist down on the table. "I thought you said that's where she was," he said as he glared at Shields, his lips quivering. "You assured me that—"

"I know you're upset," she said, "but I only promised you that the call you received which gave you proof of life was made from that location. They've obviously moved her."

"Have they? Or have they already killed her? Are we going to hear in a few hours that Miami officials recovered Morgan's body from the carnage of that explosion?"

"I hope not," Shields said. "And I doubt that's the play Sinclair would make. If your niece is dead, he has no leverage with you."

"Then where is she?" Blunt asked. "We don't have much time. If the president meets with that mastermind, we have no idea of knowing whether any decision Young makes in the future will be one that is made in the best interest of our country's national security. If Young is compromised—"

"He'll probably handle it like you have," Shields said. "Look, you can't beat yourself up about this or worry about what's going to happen next. This mission has become intensely personal for you, but we can't let that distract us from what we need to do next."

"Which is what?"

"Find Morgan," she said as she patted Blunt on the arm.

Moments later, Blunt's phone buzzed with a call. He repeated the numbers on the screen to himself before answering.

"Yeah," Blunt answered.

"Emotionless, I like it," Sinclair said. "Your niece was just obliterated, and that's all you have to say about it? I mean, who can blame you really since you're the one who's responsible for her death? I warned you not to make a rescue attempt, but you wouldn't listen to me. And here we are."

"Where is she?" Blunt asked.

"What do you mean? Weren't you watching that botched mission?" Sinclair asked.

"You're not that dumb."

"I appreciate your affirmation regarding my intelligence, but I'm also not stupid enough to tell you where we have her. You'll have to learn that on your own—but you never will if you try to pull another stunt like that again. I'll send her back to you in pieces, and I'll enjoy every minute of it."

Blunt hung up the phone and jammed it into his pocket. He needed to find Morgan before it was too late.

CHAPTER 13

Somewhere over Russia

HAWK AWOKE AS COLD AIR whooshed into his face and the cabin's air pressure vanished. He looked over at Alex, who was strapped in and unfazed by the chaos swirling around her.

"Alex," he shouted. "Alex, wake up!"

She didn't stir.

Hawk had so many questions flying through this mind, but no time to ponder any of them.

He fished his backpack from beneath his seat and fastened it around him. Next, he looked up at the overhead hatch where the parachutes were stored. Unbuckling from his seatbelt, he wrapped it around his left wrist to keep him from flying out of the door. With his right hand, he reached up and unlatched the door. Once he grabbed one of the chute straps, he pulled the pack down and carefully secured it on his back.

His next challenge was to get across the aisle and get Alex, who was still asleep. At least, he hoped she was sleeping and wasn't dead. Her unresponsiveness concerned him, but not nearly as much as the plane with an open door that was careening toward the ground.

He remained tethered to the belt and worked his way over to her.

"Alex, wake up!" he shouted.

When she didn't move, he shook her vigorously to see if she could possibly be roused.

Still nothing.

He thrust his right leg in front of her chest, pinning her against the seat while he unbuckled her. Next, he grabbed a fistful of her shirt and pulled her close to him. He held on to her with his right arm and then swung back to his side of the cabin near the door.

I hope I never wake up like she's about to.

Hawk rocked back and forth to gain enough momentum to swing out of the door. Counting to three beneath his breath, he gritted his teeth and leaped.

The air chilled Hawk to the bone. With his arms locked around Alex, he could only imagine how she might react when she awoke. He just hoped she wouldn't thrash about, though he was certain if she regained consciousness during the free fall descent, she would panic.

If Hawk had been jumping for a mission, things would be vastly different. He would know what kind of terrain he was about to land on and what he was about to face. But everything about this jump was unplanned, all the way down to Alex not having a chute and him having to cling to his wife to spare her life.

The only saving grace for Hawk was the altimeter function on his watch. Under normal circumstances, he would check it every few seconds in an attempt to time his pull perfectly. But he couldn't withstand the strain of craning his neck around Alex constantly to see his altitude. So, he had to determine the rate he was falling and estimate the right moment to yank on his rip cord. Once he felt confident, everything was thrown off when Alex opened her eyes.

"Am I dreaming?" she asked groggily as she looked around.

"Which part? The part about a dashingly handsome man saving you from the clutches of death? Or the part about you waking up in a free fall out of an airplane?"

"Both," she said.

"You are most definitely not dreaming," Hawk said.

Closing her eyes, Alex threw her head back and

screamed. When she did, her positioning made it even more difficult for Hawk to see the altimeter readout on his watch. He'd lost count but was certain the moment was nearing to deploy his parachute.

"Hold on," Hawk said before tugging on the cord.

The time it took for the parachute to unfurl seemed to last for minutes if not hours. But eventually it opened up and caught the wind, beginning their soft descent to the ground. Hawk and Alex jerked upward, halting their rapid fall.

"Are you insane?" Alex asked. "You need to give me a warning."

"I did," Hawk said. "Maybe you didn't hear me over your screaming."

"Hawk, I woke up falling out of an airplane," she said. "What other response did you expect?"

Hawk smiled, confident he could get away with a cheeky moment since the chaos was suspended for the next few minutes as they floated down to the earth.

"Don't look down," he said.

"You know how much I hate heights," she said. "I wouldn't dare dream of it."

"Good. It's going to take a while before we touch the ground again."

"What happened?" she asked.

"I have no idea," Hawk said. "When I woke up, the plane was in a free fall and the cockpit door was shut. Thank God we were both buckled in."

"So, you don't know what happened to Kip?"

Below, an explosion lit up the sky.

Hawk sighed. "I have no idea. But if he was in that cockpit, he's gone now. The plane just struck the ground."

"Hawk, where are we?"

"I'm not a hundred percent sure of that either. I can tell you one thing though: this isn't Afghanistan."

She exhaled. "That's refreshing. Waking up like that was bad enough, but then only to find out we're about to land in the middle of a village controlled by the Taliban? That would've been too much for me."

"Oh, Alex, the fun is just beginning."

"Hawk, you know where we are, don't you?"

He scanned the area, refusing to look at her. She set her jaw and glared at him.

"Hawk, where are we?"

"Based on the GPS coordinates on my watch, we're in Russia."

"Russia? How did we—"

"I have no idea what happened. After we finished working on our plan, I fell asleep—and so did you."

"I wasn't that tired," she said. "I think someone drugged me."

"Who?" Hawk said with a scowl. "And when? What did you take that could've possibly knocked you out like that?"

"I don't know, but I do know that I have a massive headache right now. And the last time my head felt like this was when someone drugged me in North Korea."

"But what did you—" Hawk stopped talking the moment he realized the source of her drug. "The water bottles."

"From Kip?" she asked. "He wouldn't do a thing like that."

"Got any other explanations? Because I was supposed to drink one of those too, but remember I didn't. And then you drank mine for me."

"That explains why I was sleeping like a dead person."

Hawk chuckled. "That's not all that different than usual. But in most cases, I will concede that you would wake up while in an airplane in a free fall with the door open."

The sound of men shouting reached Hawk's ears. He peered down over Alex's shoulders.

"What is it?" she asked.

"Oh, nothing. I was just trying to see how much longer before we hit the ground," he said.

"Stop lying to me, Hawk. I hear those guys talking. Who are they?"

"It's kind of dark, so it's difficult to tell anything for certain."

She narrowed her eyes. "Your best guess."

He winced. "I'm not going to beat around the bush on this one anymore. They're clearly Russian soldiers."

Alex shook her head slowly. "Hawk, I hope you've got a plan."

"You're assuming that they see us and are going to capture us," Hawk said.

A few seconds later, Hawk drew back and locked eyes with Alex.

"We're about to hit the ground," he said. "Just try to roll a little bit once your feet touch down so you don't break any bones."

"Roger that," she said.

"In three, two, and one . . ."

They touched down and tumbled across the ground, the parachute coming to rest on top of them. Hawk landed on his back with Alex on top of him. She smiled as she pushed herself up.

"Thanks for breaking my fall," she said.

"Any time," he said before flinging the canvas over their heads.

A bright beam shone in both their faces as the silhouette of soldiers lumbered forward.

"Keep your hands where I can see them," he bellowed.

Hawk and Alex raised their hands in a gesture of surrender.

"You're both under arrest for espionage," the commander said before nodding knowingly at some of his subordinates. They rushed over to Hawk and Alex, yanking them to their feet before dragging them toward an idling military transport vehicle.

CHAPTER 14

Washington, D.C.

BLUNT STIRRED HIS COFFEE and positioned his face over the steam. Following the unsuccessful op to rescue Morgan, he had a restless night, spent worrying about her future as well as the fate of the country. Given the lengths Falcon Sinclair had already gone through to ensure Young's attendance at this secret meeting, Blunt could only figure the fallout would be disastrous.

Blunt wrapped both hands around his "World's Best Boss" mug and took a sip. On the side of the grounds, the flavor was listed as Kenyan Bold, one of Blunt's favorites. He took the name as a sign of how he needed to lead with a master manipulator threatening his own family. This wasn't the time to hedge his bets. Sinclair was intent on gaining control on so many sectors of the world that if something wasn't done to stop him, the world would be at his mercy.

Blunt read through several reports on his desk before his administrative assistant buzzed in with a call from Randy Wood at the CIA.

"Randy, to what do I owe the pleasure of this call?" Blunt said, doing his best to sound cheery.

"I'm afraid there's going to be nothing pleasurable about this conversation."

"What is it?" Blunt asked, his voice transitioning quickly to concern.

"It's about your plane."

"My plane?"

"Yeah, the one with Hawk and Alex on it that left here last night."

"What about it?"

"It crashed in Russia last night."

"Wait. What? Russia? What was it doing in—"

"That's what I was hoping you could tell us."

Blunt set his jaw, afraid of the answer to his next question. "And Hawk and Alex?"

"Both alive," Wood said, "captured by the Russian military."

"I don't understand. How did they—"

"Actually, we were hoping you could answer some questions for us," Wood began, "starting with what the hell were they doing over Russian airspace in the first place?"

"I'm as stunned about that revelation as you are."

"What were they doing over there?"

Blunt sighed. "We used Orlovsky to set up a meeting with Evana Bahar, but apparently something went wrong."

"What about your pilot? Is he trustworthy?"

"Best in the business. He'd never get that far off course."

"So, I guess that leaves us with your operatives," Wood said. "Which one don't you trust?"

"I have—and would again—trust both of them with my life. Neither one of them would do anything like that. Maybe there was something wrong with the navigational controls. I mean, that might be able to explain a lot of things, including the crash."

"You could be right, but that still feels like quite a stretch to me. But you have a bigger problem."

"Are the Russians detaining Hawk and Alex?" Blunt asked.

"I wish your two assets were merely being detained because that'd be much easier to negotiate than what's happening now."

"Charges?"

"Yep," Wood said.

"Of what?"

"Espionage. They could face life in a work camp in Siberia or a firing squad for that offense. That's really up to the judge to decide."

"That's not even why they were there," Blunt said before growling. "Are they offering any deals?"

"Nothing that's negotiable."

"What's that supposed to mean?"

"One of the Russian generals involved in this mess also happens to be the cousin of Andrei Orlovsky," Wood said.

"So, they want to make an exchange. Why not do it? Orlovsky isn't getting us anything."

"That's not why we're holding on to him," Wood said. "The president wants to use him as Exhibit A that his administration is doing a stellar job at keeping terrorists out of this country and putting them where they belong. It's his backup plan if you can't capture Evana Bahar."

"Come on, Randy. See if you can talk to him. He won't listen to me on this issue since he knows I'm biased."

"I've already broached the subject with the president, and he was very clear about what he wanted. There's a ton of risk involved here for him. And after the attack on the White House, I don't think he's willing to go there again."

"Any other suggestions?"

"At this point, your best bet is probably an extraction team."

Blunt huffed through his nose. "You think I have

the resources for that? Are you going to help me?"

"My hands are tied. Your people knew the consequences for getting caught."

"They didn't get caught," Blunt said. "Something happened to their plane."

"If they're in Russian custody, they got caught. Now, I wish there was more I could help you with, but I'm afraid there isn't. I'll be in touch."

Blunt grunted and ended the call. Wood had always been an advocate for Blunt when he couldn't speak up for himself. But Wood's chilly response to Blunt's suggestion regarding the prisoner exchange made him wonder if his long-time ally had been compromised in some manner as well. Not that Blunt could hold any moral superiority over Wood, much less blame him.

A few minutes later, Blunt's phone buzzed with a call from the president's office.

"Senator Blunt?" a woman asked.

"Yes."

"Please hold for the President of the United States."

If Blunt wasn't awake yet, he was now, bracing for the full brunt of Young's wrath.

"J.D., I wish we were speaking under different terms," Young began.

"Believe me, Mr. President, so do I," Blunt said.

Young sighed. "Look, is there any explanation you can give me for why two of your agents were over Russia last night? I could've sworn I told you to go get Evana Bahar."

"That's what the plan was, but something happened. I'm as shocked as you are. I'm still trying to get to the bottom of it."

"What do you know so far?" Young asked.

"Probably the same amount of information as you do since I just got a call from the CIA about it."

"I'm leaving later this afternoon as part of a top-secret envoy overseas," Young said. "And when I return in four days, I want Bahar in U.S. custody or I'm shutting your little operation down so I can find someone who can get me the necessary results."

"But, sir, I've got two agents being held by the Russians now. How can you expect me to do that on such a short notice?"

"You've got other agents, don't you?"

"Yes, but—"

"Well, use them," Young said.

"I need all my agents to pull off an operation of that magnitude. And to do that, I'm going to need to make a prisoner exchange with Andrei Orlovsky."

"Out of the question. I need some scalps to wave before the American people. Have you seen the polls lately? Everybody is running around in fear for their lives here. And I can't let our citizens exist in this state for long. You're the so-called expert on this issue, so do your job and fix this."

Young hung up, and Blunt exhaled slowly. He rubbed his face and contemplated his next move.

"Screw this coffee," Blunt said as he slid his mug aside. He fished a bottle of whisky and a glass out of his drawer. Shaking his head at what he'd just heard out of the president's mouth, Blunt poured a drink and then leaned back in his chair. He knew what he needed to do, but he wasn't sure he could pull it off.

Blunt dialed Randy Wood's number and waited for the CIA's deputy director to answer.

"What's wrong now, J.D.?" Wood asked.

"Where's Orlovsky?" Blunt asked.

"He's in our Vir—" Wood cut himself off before blurting out the entire name of the secret site. "Did you talk to the president about this?"

"I did," Blunt said.

"And what did he say?"

"He told me that I've got four days to capture Evana Bahar or he's going to shut down The Phoenix Foundation."

Wood sucked a breath through his teeth. "That's rough. He can't be serious."

"Young is dead serious, trust me," Blunt said. "I've heard him give lip service about certain things, but judging from his tone, he wasn't joking. He's feeling the pressure, just like we all are."

"Well, you can't get Alex and Hawk out of there that quickly, especially without Orlovsky."

"I'm well aware of that. It's why I asked where he was."

"Look, I'm sorry you're in this situation, but there's nothing I can do for you. Orlovsky is staying put under the president's orders. And I can't lend you any of my guys as part of an extraction or op in either Russia or Afghanistan per treaty rules."

"Forget those rules," Blunt bellowed. "We've got people's lives on the line, not to mention plenty of people's livelihoods."

"I wish I could help you, J.D. I really do. But the truth is I can't lend you much support right now other than anything stateside. I know that's not what you want to hear, but we're all feeling the squeeze as we keep our ear to the ground about forthcoming threats both at home and abroad."

"I understand, but if you're willing to bend the rules a little to help me, you know where to find me," Blunt said.

"Of course. I will, J.D. We all need you to succeed."

Blunt ended the call and pocketed his phone. He got what he needed. All he had to do was put his plan into motion and hope for the best.

CHAPTER 15

Undisclosed location in Russia

HAWK WANTED TO see Alex. He needed to see her, but he could barely see anything other than the shadowy figures huddling in the corner. With his hands bound together and attached to a pole a couple feet over his head, he swayed as he strained to hear the Russian officers' conversation.

Hawk's interrogation had reached three hours. No water. No food. No break. Nothing but a relentless barrage of questions and psychological torture techniques that left him aching for a break. He could only imagine what Alex had endured, wherever she was. The moment they arrived at the military compound, the guards separated Hawk and Alex.

Over the years, he'd suffered through more than his fair share of hostile interviews from enemy combatants. Some of those "talks" required intense physical stamina just to stay conscious, much less stay mentally sharp to avoid giving up critical information. Alex had gone through the same training Hawk had, but riding out the harsh words from a man you knew and would smile and shake your hand once the exercise ended was different than being detained in a Russian prison.

A Russian officer strode in front of Hawk and glared at him. "What are you doing in Russia?"

Hawk shook his head and stuck to the script. "I'm a businessman. Our plane must have had a navigational malfunction. We were supposed to be headed to Morocco. I can show you the flight plan."

The man held up a sheet of paper. "Is this what you're referring to?"

Hawk leaned forward to read the words on the page. For instances just like this one, he always carried a fake flight plan.

"I think that's it," Hawk said as he squinted.

"This," the man said, holding up the document, "was what we retrieved from the cockpit after we put out the fire. It is a flight plan for Perm from Washington, D.C. Now, would you mind answering my question truthfully this time: What are you doing in Russia?"

"I'm not a pilot, sir," Hawk said. "I got on a plane that I thought was headed to Morocco but apparently took a turn. I don't know if there were navigational problems or what. All I can tell you is that I went to sleep and when I woke up, the plane door was open and we were in a free fall. I grabbed a parachute and my partner, and we dove out the door, hoping for the best."

The Russian officer broke into laughter. He looked around at the other men while pointing at Hawk.

"Did you all hear this?" the man said in Russian. "He expects me to believe that he's Tom Cruise starring in a Mission Impossible movie."

All the men chuckled, some of them shaking their heads at Hawk's claim.

"You better hope I'm not like Tom Cruise," Hawk said.

The man stopped and cocked his head to one side. "And why's that?"

"Because in the end, I'll escape and you'll be dead."

The officer shrugged. "Hopefully we've made more progress with your partner. But either way, it's nice to see an attractive woman around here. My men hardly know what to do with themselves when we get one."

Hawk lunged at the man but was restrained by the ropes around his wrists.

"That's right, Mr. Hawk. Get angry. Try however you wish, but understand that I'm in control here and you are powerless to do anything about it."

"You lay a finger on her and I'll gut you myself," Hawk said with a growl.

"Yet you're not in a position to do anything. What kind of relationship do you have with her anyway?"

"You're the one who seems to know so much about me, including where I was flying to. Why don't you tell me?"

The man turned on his heels and strode toward the door. "Goodbye, Mr. Hawk. I hope you enjoy our lovely accommodations here tonight. You need to get used to them because you're going to be here a while."

"Don't you touch her," Hawk said again, leaning forward in a failed attempt to run after the Russian officer. Instead, Hawk crashed headlong onto the floor, skidding to a stop.

The guards standing around him laughed as they stared. After a moment, two of them helped Hawk get upright again before ushering him into a prison cell. The sound of metal clanking together echoed down the hallway. Hawk stumbled toward his bed, his entire body weakened from the lack of sleep and sustenance.

Hawk stared at the ceiling, his mind consumed with how Alex was doing. All was quiet for a few minutes, giving him the kind of peaceful moment that he didn't desire. He wanted to know everything that was going on. If he could at least hear her, he would know if she was still alive and how they were treating her. The silence was deafening.

When the sun beamed through the slits from the small rectangular window near the ceiling, Hawk awoke. He wasn't sure how long he'd slept. Despite his concern for Alex, he'd passed out from exhaustion, unable to keep his eyes open.

He sat up and rubbed his face, his head pounding from a headache.

A guard strolled by his cell and dragged a stick across the bars. "Time to get up, American scum. We have a lot planned for you today. And what you do will determine if it's your last day with us."

"You might release me?" Hawk asked.

The man chuckled and shook his head. "No, I will put a bullet in your head if I'm given permission. And I'll enjoy it."

Another guard hustled over to the door and opened it. He gestured for Hawk to leave the cell.

"What's happening to me?" Hawk asked. "I need to know. And I need to know about my partner."

"Don't you worry about her," the first guard said. "You'll see her soon enough."

Hawk shuddered at the reply. All he wanted was a gun in his hand and enough munitions to take out every one of the smug Russians stalking about the military compound, foreign relations be damned.

Their innuendos regarding Alex made him sick—and furious.

Less than a minute later, the guards led Hawk into a common area, directing him to walk against the wall. Across the room, he saw Alex trudging forward, her feet in shackles, her hands bound by chains in front of her.

"Alex," Hawk shouted. "Are you okay?"

She slowly turned her head in the direction of his voice, but before he could see her face, the same officer who interrogated him the night before stepped in front of Hawk's line of sight.

"Mr. Hawk, it's a pleasure to see you this morning," the man said. "Did you have a chance to mull over what we talked about yesterday?"

Hawk narrowed his eyes but didn't say a thing.

"I'll take that as a yes," the officer said. "Would you like to change your story about where you were headed and what you were doing?"

"I stand by my original statement," Hawk said.

"I'm not sure that's a wise decision."

"It's the truth. I have nothing else to add."

The officer stroked his beard and eyed Hawk closely. "In that case, we have no more need for you or your partner. We contacted the American government yesterday, and they weren't willing to negotiate for either of you. Apparently, you're both expendable, not even worth a prisoner trade. So, you'll be executed tonight."

"Now, wait," Hawk said. "There might be something of value I could give you, but I need a deal in writing—and I need to see someone from the American embassy to ensure the terms of any agreement."

The officer chuckled and shook his head. "The only worth you had to us was to get back someone the U.S. recently abducted. And I doubt there's anything you could tell us that we don't already know. We have agents everywhere, Mr. Hawk."

He gestured for the guards to take Hawk away. They seized his arms and forced him in the opposite direction.

"I'm sure we could work something out," Hawk said as he struggled against their grip.

One of the guards edged up to Hawk's ear. "The only question now is who goes first: You or your wife?"

Hawk spun toward the man, jabbing him with an elbow and knocking him off balance a few feet. Once he regained his footing, he pulled out a cropping stick and whacked Hawk in the back of his legs. He crumpled, falling onto his knees.

"Get up," the man growled as he yanked Hawk by the back of his collar. "I'm going to enjoy putting you out of your misery."

For the rest of the day, Hawk oscillated between lying on his cot and pacing around his cell. All he could think about was Alex and what her situation was like. He also lamented the fact that all the intel he'd accumulated on Falcon Sinclair and Obsidian was going to go to waste. Dying by a firing squad in a Russian military facility certainly wasn't the way he expected to go out, but death was a risk he was all too aware of and something he'd flirted with many times before. He imagined if he was going to die, it'd be doing something heroic or noble, throwing himself on a bomb or sacrificing himself to save some political dignitary. But leaping out of an aircraft into the Russian's waiting arms carried quite a bit of ignominy for any spy, especially an American one.

What I'd give to be on a couch somewhere cuddled up with Alex and watching a Bollywood movie.

Hawk's druthers stood in stark contrast. He was curled up in a fetal position on a lumpy cot beneath the watchful eyes of Russian soldiers excited about filling him full of lead later that day. Even worse was the time Hawk spent waiting, though he wasn't sure if it was some psychological torture technique. If it was the latter, Hawk deemed the tactic a success.

Just after dark, a guard entered Hawk's cell with a tray of food, accompanied by an Orthodox priest.

"Would you like your last rites?" the priest asked.

Hawk nodded.

Anything to buy me more time.

The obstacle Hawk faced was that even if he had more time, he wasn't sure what he'd do with it. To escape the compound, he'd have to overcome a number of seemingly insurmountable odds, chief among them being the fact that he didn't know where Alex was. And he wasn't about to leave without her.

When the priest finished praying, Hawk looked the man in the eyes.

"Thank you," Hawk said. "At least there's one decent soul in this country."

The priest nodded. "God be with you, son."

Hawk took stock of the situation, his mind whirring with possibilities for escape. With his hands tethered in front of him, he figured he could utilize them as a weapon if he could get behind a guard and wrap them around his neck. But there were too many of them. He didn't want to go down without a fight, but there wouldn't be much of one. A bullet lodged in one of the men's guns would be lodged in Hawk's head one way or another.

Maybe dying in front of a firing squad would have some dignity to it. At least it's a noble way to go.

In an instant, his world went dark as a guard secured a blind around Hawk's head.

Moments later, he heard Alex's voice. She shrieked

and called for him.

"Hawk, don't let them do it," she cried. "Keep fighting. Keep—"

All he heard was a whack followed by a thud.

"Drag her over to the post with him," a guard said. "I wanted her to watch him die, but it's better that they do it together. And let them see one another as we shoot them."

Hawk's blindfold was removed in time for him to see Alex's limp body being dragged across the courtyard next to a wooden post positioned about six feet in front of a concrete wall. A bank of lights illuminated the outdoor space. Bullet holes served as scars from previous executions and an ominous reminder of what was merely minutes away for him and Alex.

"Talk to me, Alex," Hawk said. "Wake up."

She didn't say a word.

Hawk couldn't hold back the tears as they gushed down his face. The guards secured him to the post with her, laughing at him and mocking the American agents while doing it.

"Any famous last words?" the Russian officer in charge asked Hawk.

"This is the price of liberty and freedom," Hawk said, shouting so all the soldiers could hear him. "May you be so fortunate one day to experience it for yourselves."

The man slapped Hawk and then spit in his face. "No one will ever find your body."

Hawk took a deep breath and stood up straight. "My life speaks for itself."

"But you're about to speak no more," the officer said.

He lumbered across the field before sliding behind a row of soldiers with rifles trained on Hawk and Alex.

"Say something, Alex," Hawk said.

She was still unconscious.

"I love you," he said.

"Time for the infamous Brady Hawk to retire," the officer said. "Comrades, prepare to fire."

CHAPTER 16

"STOP!" SHOUTED A MAN charging hard into the execution area. Gasping for breath, he was waving a piece of paper in his hand. The Russian officer in charge took the document and scanned it quickly. With a sigh, he folded up the order and slid it into his jacket pocket.

"Untie them," the officer ordered in Russian.

Hawk looked at Alex, who was regaining consciousness.

"Wha—what happened?" she asked as she opened her eyes when her blindfold was removed.

"Oh, nothing," Hawk said. "Other than you and me getting thrown in front of a firing squad. That's all. Just another day at the office."

Her eyes widened. "Then how come we're still alive?"

Hawk shrugged. "Somebody halted the guards just before they were about to shoot."

"Good thing," she said. "That's not how I imagined going out."

"Me either," he said. "I didn't like the fact that I wasn't going to get to tell you goodbye."

She cocked her head to one side as guards scurried around, untying the bindings.

"Why are you looking at me like that?" Hawk asked.

"Were you crying?"

"Of course I was," he said. "The thought of seeing you like that and knowing you'd never wake up, I—"

He paused, unsure of how to end the sentence. Nothing he could think of seemed to capture the sentiments he felt for Alex. He tried again.

"It's just that—"

Alex smiled and patted him on the arm. "Sometimes there just aren't words, are there?"

Hawk shook his head. "None of them could do justice to how I feel about you."

The Russian officer strode up to them, wearing a scowl. "Apparently you are both worth something. You're to be included in a prisoner trade that will occur tomorrow."

"A prisoner trade?" Alex asked.

"That's right," he said. "Our governments agreed to terms moments before you were to be put to death. Perhaps miracles do fall out of the sky."

"What are you talking about?" Hawk asked.

"The prisoner the Americans are exchanging for both of you is my cousin, Andrei Orlovsky. And if it weren't for you, I'm quite certain I never would've seen him again. So, I have the two of you to thank for that."

Hawk tried to hide his shock. In the short time since they planned the mission to capture Evana Bahar, he understood that Orlovsky was off limits. Hawk had wanted to use Orlovsky in the operation to ensnare Bahar, but that request was denied.

"Being traded for an illegal arms dealer is not something I want to be thanked for," Hawk said.

"Watch your tongue, Mr. Hawk. We still have plenty of time with you before the exchange. And how you spend those hours is up to me."

"If you want me to grovel at your feet, you can forget it."

The officer pulled his jacket taut and nodded at the guards. "Put him in the hole. And leave the woman with me."

Hawk resisted the guards' prodding as they shoved him forward. "I will hunt you down and kill you if you touch her."

"Enough," Alex said as another pair of soldiers ushered her away.

Hawk didn't make it easy for the men to take him back to "the hole," fighting them every step of the way. When they arrived, he understood the reason why it was called a hole. One of the guards lifted a round cover, revealing a dark space. Hawk peered inside but couldn't tell where the bottom was. Before he could say a word, one of the men used his foot to shove Hawk in the butt, sending him tumbling head over heels into the hole.

Hawk hit the ground with his left shoulder, resulting in an immediate ache.

The guards laughed as they slammed the hatch shut and walked away.

Hawk wasn't amused by any of it. He should've kept his mouth shut, and he knew it. He'd endangered Alex with his mouth, though he knew she could deal with anyone on her own. But he couldn't excuse himself for such behavior.

He spent the next two hours beating himself up for his interaction with the Russian. But the ruing ended abruptly when two guards called down into the darkness for him.

"Come with us," one of the men said.

Hawk looked up, unsure of how to proceed. Before he could ask, one of the men shone a light into the area, revealing a ladder attached to the side of the wall and leading up to the cover.

Hawk didn't need explicit instructions, scaling to the surface. The guards led him down a series of corridors where he was reunited with Alex.

"Did he touch you?" Hawk asked.

She shook her head. "He was just rattling your cage. And you fell for it. You're better than that."

Hawk sighed and nodded. Alex was right, and he needed to keep his composure, despite the intense pressure he felt from every aspect of his life.

"I'm sorry," he said. "I should've held my temper."

"You're a good man, Brady Hawk. Just don't let that fiery attitude be the death of you, okay? You've got enough people taking aim at you that you don't need to make yourself an even bigger target. Besides, I can handle myself, and I think you know that by now."

Hawk nodded, refusing to shy away from the criticism. The pressure had taken its toll, but he knew that relief wasn't coming any time soon. He needed to focus and prepare for what was coming next.

As they rounded the corner, Hawk looked up to see J.D. Blunt flanked by Titus Black and Andrei Orlovsky. Blunt exchanged a few words with Russian officials before Hawk and Alex were shoved in the back toward the direction of The Phoenix Foundation director.

"You better hope I never catch you again," the Russian officer said.

Hawk resisted the urge to snipe back at the man,

instead choosing to make a mental note of the man's face and commit it to memory. If they ever met again, Hawk wouldn't take the man as a prisoner. The score would be settled in a different manner.

Hawk looked at Blunt, bags heavy beneath his eyes. His dour expression wasn't out of the ordinary, but the edges of his lips seemed turned downward more than usual. Blunt didn't speak until they had all exited the compound and were inside the car.

"What the hell happened here?" Blunt said.

"It's a story with a lot of holes," Hawk said.

"You better start filling them in," Blunt said as he adjusted the rearview mirror in order to see Hawk and Alex.

Titus Black ignited the engine and eased onto the accelerator as they bumped along the road leading away from the facility.

"From the best I can tell, someone sabotaged the plane," Hawk said before recounting what he knew about the situation.

"What about you, Alex?" Blunt asked. "What do you recall?"

"Not much," she said, "other than waking up with Hawk holding onto me and telling me not to look down. I wish I knew more, but I just don't. We think someone drugged me."

"Captain Covington?" he asked.

"It was either him or the co-pilot," she said. "But I never interacted with him other than to say hello when I arrived at the hangar."

"Well, none of that matters now," Blunt said. "We just need to get home as soon as possible and figure out a way to deal with the impending mess Sinclair is about to make when he coopts President Young."

* * *

AN HOUR LATER, the wheels were up and they were soaring over Russia, leaving the country behind. Hawk had plenty of unfinished business in the massive country, business that didn't even pertain to the officer who'd treated them so poorly. But that would all have to wait. The more pressing matter centered around President Young's impending meeting with Falcon Sinclair.

Blunt gave Alex a laptop, pre-loaded with all her files that were backed up from the CIA's server farm. As the team discussed a strategy for preventing Sinclair from coopting Young, Hawk became annoyed with Blunt's insistence that the president and the tech billionaire meet.

"You can sway Young to cancel the meeting," Hawk said.

"It's too late," Blunt said. "That ship has sailed,

both figuratively and literally. Young wouldn't tell me much about his meeting, other than the details were secret. But one of my White House insiders told me that Young was flying to Kuala Lumpur and sailing out of Port Klang on one of Sinclair's high-speed yachts."

"And where were they going?" Alex asked.

"That's the part my informant didn't know. Apparently, not even Young knew."

"So, Young is floating around at sea with some Australian billionaire he just met?" Hawk asked. "That doesn't seem like the wisest thing."

"His Secret Service detail is with him," Blunt said. "But I'd feel much better if we knew what exactly Sinclair was up to because it can't be good."

Hawk sighed and shook his head. "I would've felt much better if you had stopped Young from ever meeting Sinclair in the first place."

"Young insisted on it, saying that the location was secret because Sinclair had some world-changing technology that he wanted to demo," Blunt said.

"We need to figure out where they're meeting so we can find out what this big secret is," Hawk said.

Blunt shook his head. "No, we need to find Evana Bahar so we don't lose funding."

Hawk pounded his fist onto the arm of his chair. "If Obsidian turns Young into a puppet, what difference does it make if we have funding or not. We'll never be able to do what we need to do to keep America safe from terrorists. Instead, we might just be letting a coup take place while we chase after some terrorist so the president can pound his chest about how safe we are as a country. Meanwhile, he'll be inviting the worst kind of terror to the White House, the kind of terror you have no idea even exists and is poisoning everything you ever believed in. I, for one, don't want that on my conscience."

Alex raised her hand as she stared at her computer screen. "Uh, guys, I just got an email from Helenos-9."

"The hacker in Berlin?" Hawk asked. "What does he want?"

"He said that there's something he needs to tell us—in person," Alex said.

"We don't have time for that," Blunt said. "We need to go to Morocco and plan how we're going to capture Evana Bahar."

Hawk scowled. "What's wrong with you, sir? About a week ago, you were convinced our highest priority was stopping Obsidian and not Bahar and Al Fatihin. This about-face from you is puzzling."

"Staying in Young's good graces is important for the future of this organization, one that I feel strongly has a vital role in the country's security both now and in the future. I don't want to jeopardize everything we've built because we're suspicious of Sinclair's motives."

"Suspicious of his motives?" Alex asked as she furrowed her brow. "We know he's scheming to seize power in every sector possible. And if we're serious about securing our country, we need to take this threat far more seriously than any bomb Evana Bahar's minions can sneak into the country. We're talking about the fabric of our democracy at stake here with what Sinclair wants to do."

"Okay, fine," Blunt said. "I guess maybe we can stop for fuel in Berlin," Blunt said. "But we can't stay long. We can keep working on that while we pursue Bahar."

Hawk cast a sideways glance at Alex. He could tell she was wary of Blunt's emphatic push to get the terrorist leader.

Something's not right.

Then something on Alex's screen grabbed her attention.

"Whoa," she said. "Now this is interesting."

"What is it?" Hawk asked, leaning over to look at her screen.

"I just saw a post on one of the chatrooms on the dark web that I follow. Helenos-9 is dead."

"Then who sent you that message?" Blunt asked.

"I don't know," she said. "But we're going to find out."

CHAPTER 17

Berlin, Germany

ALEX PUSHED THE DOORBELL and waited for someone to answer at Becketts Kopf, the eclectic cocktail bar selected for the meeting with Helenos-9. Eventually a woman draped in an apron welcomed Alex inside. When she responded that she would rendezvous with the infamous hacker, she expected going to a dive. But this place felt more like a millionaire's study than a spot to throw back a few drinks and unwind after a long day at work. Plush leather chairs and wood trimming throughout the building belied the quirky nature of using a buzzer to gain access to the establishment.

"Are you meeting someone?" the woman asked.

Alex nodded as she scanned the tables. "I don't see him yet, but I can wait at the bar."

"Why don't I seat you?" the woman said with a warm smile. "I'm sure your friend will be along soon enough—and I wouldn't want to have you get stuck talking to Peter, unless you're into football, in which case you'll find him engaging and informative.

Alex forced a grin. "I'll take that table."

Once she took a seat, the woman handed Alex a menu, disguised as a Samuel Beckett novel. After finding the drink list buried in the back, she ordered a Sazerac and perused through the German translation of *Murphy*.

"Any sign of him yet?" Hawk asked.

She covered her mouth so no one could see her talking to herself. "Negative."

"If you can, make one more sweep of the place so we can capture the faces of everyone in there and run them through some facial recognition software," Hawk said.

"Roger that," Alex said, keeping her hand over her mouth nonchalantly.

Alex complied with Hawk's request and rotated in her chair, allowing the camera hidden in her broach to register all the faces.

"Got it," Hawk said.

Alex returned to perusing the pages in front of her, while casting furtive glances in all directions whenever she noticed significant movement out of the corner of her eyes. However, no one even closely resembled Helenos-9. After she received her drink, she took a sip and noted that not a single male was sitting alone in Becketts Kopf.

"Where is he?" she muttered to herself.

While she was staring at the words on the page, the voice of a woman interrupted Alex's train of thought.

"Excuse me, but is this seat taken?" a young woman asked.

Alex hesitated. "Actually, I was waiting on a friend."

"I'm sorry," the woman said. "The person you were waiting on didn't happen to be this man, did it?"

She flashed her phone screen at Alex, revealing an image of Helenos-9. The image startled her at first, but then she scowled, unsure if she needed to say the code word for Hawk so he would storm in.

"I'm sorry, but do I know you?" Alex asked.

The young, bespectacled woman eased into the seat on the opposite side of the table. She wore a dark pant suit and with a royal-blue blouse, while her hair was pulled up into a tight bun. Holding her phone in one hand, she clung to the strap of a computer bag with the other.

"Sorry to approach you like this, but it's how I'm now forced to conduct business," she said.

Alex furrowed her brow. "What business do I have with you?"

"I'm sorry. Where are my manners?" she said, extending her hand. "I'm Helenos-9."

Alex stared at the woman's hand before glancing back at her. "I'm afraid you're not who I'm looking for."

The woman chuckled. "Oh, but you are. I'm sure you're asking yourself right now, 'I thought Helenos-9 was a man.' And you'd more or less be right. The public persona of Helenos-9 was my brother, Dietrich. But he's sadly no longer with us, likely because of how he handled the information you gave him."

"Are you suggesting I had something to do with his death?" Alex asked.

"*Murder*," the woman corrected. "And, no, I'm not. You're just not aware of all the facts, starting with the fact that my brother was never a hacker."

"Come again."

"I said, my brother was never a hacker. I was always the one behind the scenes doing all the dirty work. He was just the public front for our little enterprise."

"So, let me get this straight," Alex said. "You are the brains of the operation and used your brother as the front man for your hacking business."

"That's a perfect summation, Mrs. Hawk," she said. "Perhaps if this espionage job doesn't work out for you, you'll be able to find something in the world of public relations."

Alex chuckled. "If this espionage thing doesn't work out, it means I'm dead."

"Just like my brother," the woman said. "My name is Mia, by the way."

"How do I know you're telling the truth?" Alex asked.

"Maybe because I have corresponded with you multiple times in the past, most recently calling you Cowgirl in one of my emails."

"That doesn't mean anything. You could've hacked into Helenos-9's files."

"I don't consider what I do hacking when I have the password," she said. "At that point, it's just harvesting information."

"What are you trying to say?"

Mia sighed. "Do I have to spell it out for you, from one hacker to another?"

"You're—" Alex covered her mouth as the reality dawned on her.

"Yeah, I'm Helenos-9," Mia said. "My brother was never a great hacker, but he was far better at dealing with people than I was. But his greed spelled his ultimate demise."

"So, he wasn't a hacker?"

"He thought he was, but I ran circles around him.

I don't even think he tried to crack your files. But I know he tried to cover his tracks and keep me from seeing what he did with you. And since he was the public face of Helenos-9, when he agreed to work with Falcon Sinclair, that was the end of everything, including his life."

"He didn't commit suicide?" Alex asked.

"It sure did look like it, but my brother was such a narcissist that he'd never do anything like that. Falcon Sinclair's goons staged the scene. But there's no doubt that they murdered him."

"And do they know about you?"

Mia shook her head. "I'm just his live-in sister who worked at a coffee shop during the day and had no knowledge of his business dealings."

"Is this why you wanted to meet, to tell me what really happened?"

"Quite the contrary. I wanted to give you the information you expected to get."

"And what's that?" Alex asked.

"Everything that's on this flash drive has been unlocked and is open for your viewing pleasure. I hope you accept this as my apology for what my bother did."

Alex furrowed her brow. "What exactly did he do?"

"He told Sinclair about your meeting and then

passed along phony information."

"I'm surprised you're helping me considering that I'm part of the U.S. government."

"You won't be when you see what's on there."

Alex held up the device. "What am I going to find on here?"

"The truth about what Sinclair wants to do to the world—dominate every sector of it and control humanity. Based on what I've read about him and his philosophy about the planet and human population, he believes that if he can control everything, he can make the world a better place. But his proposals are draconian and will amount to most people being little more than slaves."

"That's all in here?" Alex asked.

"None of that is," Mia said. "That's just what I've gathered over the past few years from following him. What you'll find on there is his means of accomplishing this end."

"And what's that?" Alex asked.

"You need to see it for yourself. I can't really describe the magnitude of the weapon he's built and the way he intends to use it."

"What are you talking about?"

"It's all on there," Mia said, nodding at the thumb drive in Alex's hand.

"Why are you doing this?" Alex asked. "You know

that, in a roundabout way, I work for the U.S. government."

"Yeah, but this is a fight we must all take up against Falcon Sinclair. You'll see what I mean when you sift through the files. If he gets his way, we're all in trouble, every last human on the planet."

"Thank you," Alex said, clutching the memory stick in her hand. "I knew your brother, and he was a good man."

"No, he wasn't," Mia said. "He put up a good front, but don't lionize him. He was a greedy bastard who only thought about himself, especially in this instance. And unfortunately, that's why he's dead today."

Alex dug her laptop out of her bag and inserted the flash drive.

"I'm not sure you want to do that here," Mia said. "If anyone else sees this—"

"Just make sure they don't. There's too much at stake right now. I don't have any time to lose."

"Okay," Mia said. "I understand. And you're right. He plans to demonstrate that weapon in two days."

"Where?"

"It's all in there," Mia said.

"*Where* exactly?" Alex asked again.

Mia shrugged. "I didn't take the time to look up the coordinates, but it's all right there."

Alex's mouth gaped as she stared at the screen revealing the schematics of what Sinclair had created. "This is unbelievable."

"Believe it," Mia said. "If he unleashes this thing, we're all going to be bowing down to him and kissing his feet."

"Not if I have anything to say about it," Alex said.

"Good luck. You're going to need it."

Alex cocked her head to one side. "What are you talking about?"

"I've been researching about that island for quite a few years now, trying to figure out what Sinclair was doing. It's got one of the tightest cybersecurity systems in the world."

"Do you have any plans for the next few days?" Alex asked.

"Well, I—"

"Good," Alex said. "Go home and grab a bag and throw some clothes in it. You're coming with me."

CHAPTER 18

Port Klang, Malaysia

PRESIDENT YOUNG DREW a deep breath before boarding Falcon Sinclair's luxury liner. The frenetic pace of loading and unloading of cargo ships nearby stood in stark contrast to the serene water surrounding the boat. Young squinted as he peeked at the sun, which was still climbing. While he knew the trip was short, he appreciated the opportunity to escape Washington's constant pressure cooker, even if his presence in this part of the world was still business related.

"A fine day to set sail, isn't it?" Sinclair asked as he threw his arm around Young.

"Any day in the water is a good day by my standards," he said, a faint smile appearing on his lips.

"From what I understand about American politics, any day not spent in Washington is a good day."

Young chuckled. "That's not far from the truth.

There are days when I feel like I'm mired on a sinking ship full of rats and snakes."

"Sounds like a family dinner at my former in-laws, emphasis on former there."

Young nodded as if he understood but didn't say a word.

"Oh, I'm sorry," Sinclair said. "That was rather insensitive of me. I'm sure after the ordeal you've just been through that you'd probably give almost anything to be back at your in-laws for a meal with Madeline. Please forgive me. I—"

"No need to apologize. And to be honest, between you and me, never having to endure another one of their family functions again is the only thing that brings me joy when I think about Madeline being gone."

"I lost half my fortune to divorce my wife Kitty, and I have to say it was money well spent. I don't have to listen anymore to her father and mother discuss high society and bicker over which spoon we're supposed to use for soup versus tea. Mindless banter like that is enough to make any man want to leap out of a window."

Young ran his hand along the leather seat and shook his head. "From the looks of things, I don't think your bottom line has been affected much."

"Not at all," Sinclair said. "Since Kitty left, I've

been far more productive and have managed to find time for profitable projects that were merely untouched ideas. It's amazing how women can hold you back."

Young bristled at the comment but didn't say anything. He loved Madeline and never saw her high maintenance ways as a hindrance to his ability to perform at a high level. Without her, he felt his motivation waning. But he wasn't interested in quarreling with Sinclair over his views on women, especially considering that Sinclair promised to demonstrate a new piece of technology that could be vital as it pertained to keeping Americans safe.

"So, when are we going to leave port?" Young asked in an effort to change topics.

"Soon, I hope," Sinclair said, ushering Young below deck. "We're still waiting on some more participants for this demonstration, but they should be here any minute now."

Young furrowed his brow. "Other participants?"

"Oh, yes, that must've slipped my mind," Sinclair said as he shut the door behind him. "I'm a businessman. You didn't think you were the only government I'm courting with this technology, did you?"

Young narrowed his eyes. "Who else is joining us?"

Sinclair winked. "Don't worry. You'll get along just fine with this gentleman. In fact, I think the two of you might have more in common than you think."

"Who is it?" Young asked, his tone measured and firm.

A knock at the door delayed Sinclair's response. "Why don't I just show him to you?" Sinclair asked as he strode across the room. He tugged on the handle of the door and opened it, revealing one of the guests Sinclair was referring to.

Young stared slack-jawed at the man for a moment before speaking. "You must be joking."

Standing at the door with a glass tumbler in his hand was Russian president Dmitry Karelin. He scowled and glared at the US president before turning his attention toward Sinclair.

"You didn't mention that *he* would be here," Karelin said, pointing at Young as he entered the room.

The door slammed behind him as the engines whined. With the ship lurching forward, Young reached for the back of a nearby chair to steady himself. Once his feet were firmly on the ground, he moved toward Sinclair.

"What kind of sick joke is this?" Young asked.

"I can assure you, Mr. President, this is no joke," Sinclair said. "I'm all business, particularly when it comes to these sorts of demonstrations."

Young edged closer to Sinclair, getting within inches as the two men went nose to nose. "Where are we going?"

"Calm down," Sinclair said as he backed away. "Don't get your knickers in a bunch. I have no intention of bringing any harm to either of you while aboard this ship. Both of your security details are with us, and it'd be lunacy to do anything other than endear myself to you."

"Springing Karelin on me does nothing of the sort," Young said. "In fact, a move like that does quite the opposite."

Sinclair wagged his finger at Young. "You Americans are the absolute worst at making hasty judgments. Why don't you inquire about all the facts of this endeavor before casting judgments and storming off with your empty threats? You know good and well that if anything I have will benefit your country, you'll be begging for it."

Karelin smirked at Young and shook his head. "Mr. President, this is exactly why you don't understand the finer points of diplomacy."

"That's rich coming from you," Young said with a sneer. "Bulldozing your way around Eastern Europe seems to lack the subtle nuances of negotiations."

"There's a time to deal and a time to fight," Karelin

said. "And right now is a time to listen."

"Did you know I'd be here?" Young asked.

"I've learned to expect the unexpected with Mr. Sinclair. He's always sure to surprise with whatever he's doing."

"I'm not fond of *this* type of surprise," Young snapped.

"Gentlemen, everything will be made clear in due time," Sinclair said. "In the meantime, have a drink from my bar over here and relax. We have about a twelve-hour voyage ahead of us."

"Where are we going?" Young asked.

"That, too, is a surprise, but you'll find out soon enough," Sinclair answered with a wink.

* * *

AFTER SETTLING INTO his cabin on Sinclair's yacht, Young and his Secret Service agents discussed how they would handle the situation, now full of unknowns. The leader of the security detail recommended that they get a helicopter to get him off the boat as soon as possible, an idea that Young wasn't totally opposed to. But he didn't want any new technology that Sinclair was peddling to fall into the hands of the Russians without at least knowing what it was capable of doing. After bandying about several ideas, the consensus was that if Young must stay, the team must be vigilant and not allow the president into any room without first sweeping it. Young agreed to the terms, though he wasn't entirely sure he would abide by them.

Young passed the time by reading over secured documents on his laptop and writing up proposals for several new initiatives he wanted Congress to address in the coming year. It was busy work to keep his mind off the endless possibilities of what Falcon Sinclair was about to demonstrate for both him and Karelin—or, for that matter, where they were going. Young had studied a map for hours on the flight to Kuala Lumpur and couldn't for the life of him pinpoint a location.

Young took a short nap and awoke to a knock on the door from one his Secret Service agents. "Sir, Mr. Sinclair is here to see you."

Young rolled out of bed before lumbering toward the door.

"Is it time?" Young asked before peeking at his watch.

Sinclair nodded. "We're docking into port as we speak. Have your men ready as we're about to go ashore."

Ten minutes later, Young exited the cabin and reached the deck followed by Karelin and both their security teams. Night had fallen hours ago, and the sky glittered with stars on the moonless night. A cool breeze whipped across Young's face, while nearby palm trees rustled.

"Where are we?" Young asked.

"It's certainly not Washington," Karelin cracked. "I don't smell a stench."

"That only happens when Congress is in session," Young snapped.

Karelin chuckled. "Still pitching yourself as a man of the people, I see."

"If the shoe fits," Young said.

"Your country is so gullible," Karelin scoffed.

"At least our government tells its citizens the truth."

Karelin snickered. "Delusion is a terrible thing, comrade."

Young ignored Karelin and walked up the ramp onto the dock where Sinclair was waiting for them.

"Welcome to the Andaman Islands, and, more precisely, Rutland Island," Sinclair said. "I trust that you'll enjoy your accommodations this evening before we reconvene in the morning. I will be riding with you all on this bus and be happy to answer any questions you might have. So, gentlemen, comrades, is there anything you'd like to know?"

"What exactly are we going to see tomorrow?" Young asked.

"That will have to wait until after you've both had a good night of sleep."

* * *

YOUNG DIDN'T APPRECIATE all of Sinclair's theatrics, but there was no argument that the living quarters were worthy of kings and presidents. Marble floors, mahogany walls, hand-crafted leather couches—Young made a note to inquire about Sinclair's designer before the morning meetings.

The White House sure could use a facelift.

The Secret Service agents scurried ahead of Young as he toured the rooms. Once the security detail gave him the signal that the place was clear, Young settled in for the evening. And by 10:30 p.m., he was fast asleep.

When he awoke, he was treated to a hearty breakfast before Sinclair ushered all his guests across the property to a building hidden in one of Rutland Island's natural rain forest habitats.

"I didn't know the Indian government allowed foreigners to inhabit this island," Young said.

Sinclair smiled and winked at Young. "With enough money, anything is possible. And in this case, all it took was installing a pipeline to bring fresh water here along with establishing a power unit. We needed both of those things for our laboratory anyway."

"You do research here?" Karelin asked.

"Quite a bit, actually," Sinclair said. "By conducting our business in such a manner, we avoid outside prying eyes, corporate spies, and blatant lies."

"Sounds reasonable," Karelin said.

"It's the only way I operate. Life is too short for someone to steal your ideas and profit off them. Sadly, that's the world we live in today, and I won't apologize for taking every precaution to prevent that from happening."

Sinclair hustled up the steps and glanced over his shoulder at his party. He walked over to a black box to the right of the front door and depressed his forehead against it. A red laser scanner moved across his face before the screen flashed green and the door unlocked.

"Now, if you'll wait just inside," Sinclair said as he swung the door open and held it for his guests. "I'll give you a brief primer, and we'll get started."

Young, Karelin, and the rest of Sinclair's entourage congregated in the narthex, awaiting the billionaire's next instructions. He gestured toward one of the doors before walking up to it. He placed his face in front of another facial recognition scanner.

"State of the art security for some of our more sensitive rooms here," Sinclair announced as he opened the door.

But when Young's Secret Service team attempted to go inside first, Sinclair slid in front of them, blocking their way.

"Excuse me," one of the agents said. "We need to sweep this room first."

Sinclair didn't budge. "There are only two people allowed in that room besides me—and that's President Young and President Karelin. So, if you'll kindly step aside so they can join me, I'd be most grateful."

"If we don't go inside, he doesn't go inside," the agent said with a growl.

"Fine," Sinclair said. "I'll just take the Russian president. Thank you for your time. You're free to go."

Young pushed his way past his guard. "I'll be fine. Just stay out here and wait for me."

The agent relented, stepping back with a sigh. Young gave the man a reassuring nod.

"This is not what we agreed upon," the agent said.

"I know, but it's okay. Mr. Sinclair isn't going to do anything reckless. And neither is President Karelin. It's just a cordial meeting. Now, carry on."

Young wasn't sure he believed the words coming out of his mouth, but he couldn't stand the thought of Sinclair showing off a piece of high-tech weaponry without at least knowing what his enemies had in their possession. He wasn't entirely convinced that this was a simple demonstration, but he was confident that

Sinclair wouldn't do something to jeopardize his fortune.

Once they were all inside, the door locked behind them, the room rotated ninety degrees, and it then sank beneath ground level.

"What's happening?" Karelin asked.

"Nothing to worry about," Sinclair said. "We just need to move to a more secure portion of the building."

A half-minute later, the room came to a stop and the windows revealed that the trio of men were standing in a control center overlooking a warehouse floor. Below them, dozens of workers clad in all black outfits occupied computer terminals, communicating with one another while they typed.

"What are we looking at here?" Young asked.

"Welcome to the Janus Control Center," Sinclair said as he swept his hand past the large plate-glass window. "Everyone down there has been preparing diligently for the past six months in anticipation of your arrival."

Young raised an eyebrow. "Did you say six months?"

Sinclair nodded. "Probably longer, but about that amount of time."

"I didn't even know I was going to be here until a few days ago," Young said. "How could you know that we would show up?"

"All I had to do was invite you."

"But I didn't even know you. We only recently met at my wife's—"

Young stopped as he started to extrapolate out the potential implication of this revelation.

"Stop reading too much into my explanation," Sinclair said. "I was only trying to give you an idea that my team here has been working tirelessly to show you something that's going to change the world, one way or another."

"What's that supposed to mean?" Young asked.

"You'll see what I'm talking about soon enough," Sinclair said before he leaned toward a console and spoke into the microphone.

"Do you know what he's about to show us?" Young asked Karelin.

He shook his head. "But whatever it is, I want it."

Sinclair pressed a button on the panel in front of him and addressed his workers one more time. "The time has come. Initiate the launch protocol."

CHAPTER 19

**Two Hours Earlier
Off the coast of
Rutland Island, Indian Ocean**

HAWK DIDN'T MOVE as the dive instructor began his spiel about how to operate the oxygen tanks. The boat rocked back and forth just off shore. The man stormed over to Hawk and leaned down, getting in his face.

"This is the most important thing I will tell you all day," the man said. "If you don't listen, you may die."

Hawk eyed the man before standing up, towering over him. "I'm not diving."

"You're not what?" the man asked, his eyes widening. "You paid two hundred dollars for me to guide you on a dive."

"None of us are diving," Hawk said, nodding toward Alex and Mia. "I'll pay you a thousand dollars to beach this boat over there."

The man scowled as he looked at Hawk. "We don't have a permit."

"You can leave us there," Hawk said. "We'll find our way back."

"I can't do that, I—"

"Two thousand dollars," Hawk said.

"Okay, okay. I'll do it."

The instructor hustled to the back of the boat and raised the anchor. Moments later, he was steering the vessel toward the shore.

Hawk handed the man a stack of cash. "There's an extra thousand in there for keeping your mouth shut. If you talk, I'll know it."

The man nodded as he took the money. "Not a word, my friend. Good luck on the island."

Hawk, Alex, and Mia lugged all their equipment off the boat and trudged across the sand. They found a shaded spot just beyond the shoreline and set up camp.

"Are we sure this is the spot?" Mia asked.

"If you decoded that flash drive properly, it is," Hawk said. "If not, we've gone out of our way to spend an odd day at the beach."

"No, this is it," Alex said. "When I entered in the coordinates to check out the location from the NSA's satellite feed a few hours ago, there's no question that this is the place."

"So, what's the plan?" Mia asked. "Or more to the point, why am I here?"

"We need your hacking skills," Alex said. "If Falcon Sinclair is going to demonstrate that new weapon of his, we need to be in position to shut it down. And I'd rather have one of the world's best hackers working with me than not."

"I'll do whatever you need," Mia said. "After I saw what that weapon can do, I'll do anything to stop it."

"Good," Hawk said. "That's the kind of attitude we need to get the job done."

Alex finished setting up her remote satellite dish, enabling her to communicate with the NSA's computers as well as get online and utilize their com links. Hawk set up a perimeter alarm in case they had any unwanted visitors. While he didn't like the idea of Alex working on a remote island with unknown inhabitants, he didn't have much of a choice given the situation.

Once they were done, Alex logged on. Her mouth gaped as she stared at her screen.

"What is it?" Hawk asked.

"It looks like Sinclair is preparing to demonstrate the weapon. They are moving rockets to the launch site."

Hawk let out a string of expletives as he paced around the tent. "Can you stop them?"

"Not unless I have a direct connection," Alex said.

"And how are we going to do that?"

"We need to change our plans," she said. "Storming the facility and sabotaging the missiles isn't going to work now. It's too late."

"What do you suggest?" he asked.

"I need you to plant a transmitter on the rockets," Alex explained. "If you do that, I should be able to hack into the weapon's mainframe and divert it before we witness a brazen attack."

"You really think Falcon Sinclair would aim these missiles at a highly populated city?" Mia asked.

Hawk shrugged. "I sure as hell don't want to find out the hard way. This guy is already controlling so many market sectors that we're all subject to him whether we realize it or not. If he's able to become a confidant to the U.S. president, we're all in trouble."

"Can't argue with that reasoning," Mia said.

Hawk crammed the com link device into his ear and then looked at Alex. "I need you to guide me to the rockets."

"I'll do my best," she said. "Better get going. You don't have any time to lose."

Hawk took a few steps toward the tent door before he turned around and marched back over to her. He gave her a hug and kissed her.

"Get a room," Mia said after the prolonged lip lock.

Hawk pulled back and then smiled before glancing

at Mia. "Trust me. I fully intend to once this whole ordeal is settled."

He winked at Alex before darting outside and into the rain forest that covered the island. After starting with a swift jog, he increased his pace. Upon breaking into a full sprint, his lungs burned. His quads ached as he extended his stride.

"You're making good time," Alex said over the coms. "Keep it up. You'll be there before you know it."

Hawk wanted to respond, but he needed to save his breath. He pumped his arms and kept his eyes affixed on a gray building in the distance.

"Up ahead, take a left," Alex said. "I can't tell how clear it is to you, but there appears to be a path approaching that will lead you directly to the launch site."

"Roger that," Hawk said as he scanned the route for a path that veered off to the left.

After about fifty meters, he spotted a clearing on the left that looked like it turned off the main thoroughfare.

"Going left," he announced. "Does this look right to you?"

Hawk slowed his pace a bit as he waited for confirmation from Alex. Her feed was a couple seconds behind him.

"That's the one," she said. "Keep going. You're about a half-mile from the perimeter."

Hawk resumed his torrid pace and rushed up to the fence.

"Talk to me, Alex. What do you see?"

"Looks like the coast is clear," she said. "The rockets appear to be loaded onto a vehicle that's slowly making its way to the launch site. I can't tell if anyone is actually driving."

Hawk pulled his binoculars out of his rucksack and then zeroed in on the front of the vehicle.

"How's it look from the ground?" she asked.

"I think the launch vehicle is remote controlled."

"Still be careful as you approach it, Hawk. Even though Sinclair might feel like he's safe in the middle of nowhere, he's no fool. This place is covered with cameras. As soon as you attach the transmitter to the vehicle, run like hell. Mia and I will take care of the rest."

"Roger that," Hawk said.

He dug the magnetized box containing the device out of his pocket with his left hand. In his right, he carried a Glock. The launch area was a clearing about a hundred square meters and surrounded by a twelve-foot steel fence topped with barbed wire. After surveying the area one final time, Hawk shimmied up the fence and hurtled over it, hitting the ground hard but rolling to the side to lessen the impact. Darting to his feet, he sprinted toward the vehicle.

When he was about thirty yards away from his target, he noticed two armed men barreling toward him at full speed. Hawk veered to his left, changing the duo's angle to give him a chance to reach his destination. He fired a couple shots, but they failed to hit either of the men. As he closed in on the launcher, he realized that he wasn't going to make it.

Instead of getting gunned down, Hawk slowed down and threw his hands in the air, dropping his gun. The pair of men kept their guns trained on him.

"What do you want me to do with him?" one of the guards asked on his coms.

After a brief moment, he responded. "Roger that."

"Kick that weapon over here, pal," the other guard said as Hawk promptly complied.

"Today's your lucky day," the other guard said. "You're not going to die—yet."

Hawk sighed and put his head down as the launcher passed less than a foot behind him.

"Oh, Hawk, don't get yourself killed," Alex said over the coms.

Hawk placed his hands behind his back and waited for the men to bind him.

CHAPTER 20

ALEX PACED AROUND the tent and contemplated her next move. With Hawk in custody, stopping the rockets from firing would be an impossible challenge. She and Mia simply didn't have the time required to hack into Sinclair's system and thwart the launch.

As Alex weighed all her options, Mia pumped her fist while staring at one of the laptop screens.

"Get over here, Alex," she said. "We have work to do."

Alex sighed. "Yeah, but not even you are good enough to crack the firewall Sinclair has here."

"I don't need to. Hawk came through."

Alex rushed over to Mia's computer and gaped at the information scrolling across the screen. From the satellite image, she never saw Hawk place the magnetic device on the rocket launcher, but based on Mia's progress, he obviously had.

"When did he do that?" Alex asked.

"He must've slipped the transmitter on there when

it rolled past him," Mia said. "That's the only time he got near enough to do it."

Breaking into the rocket's onboard computer was far simpler than fighting through an entire computer system protected by layers of security. The weapons relayed information with the control center and were presumed to be safe from outside interference. That is, unless someone had a way of communicating directly with the rockets. Alex and Mia now had a way.

The duo hammered away on their laptops, breaking through the simple defenses on the rockets' mainframes and rewriting the way the weapons would communicate. They passed information back and forth, focusing on the task at hand. She still wasn't convinced they had enough time to circumvent the mainframe, viewing the mission as a long shot. But as long as there was still time, she was going to keep working. If she and Mia didn't establish a connection before the rockets were launched, there was little chance that the mission would be accomplished.

Alex's fingers were flying as she worked on the code. However, she stopped when she heard one of the guards talking over Hawk's coms.

"Sinclair wants to see him and make an example out of him," the guard said.

Alex winced, worried that she'd never see Hawk again.

"We need to get a move on," the guard said. "They're about to fire up these rockets."

* * *

SINCLAIR GROWLED as he studied the scene in the launch area through his binoculars.

"I apologize for the delay, gentlemen," he said. "It appears as though someone is attempting to sabotage my demonstration."

"There's someone out there?" Young asked as he moved toward the window.

"It's difficult to believe, I know," Sinclair said, "especially given how impossible it is to get on this island. But some nut job found a way and is trying to subvert my plans."

He watched as two of his security agents corralled the man.

"Okay, looks like the problem has been resolved," Sinclair announced. "My security team has apprehended the man, and we're now safe to resume the launch sequence."

Sinclair placed his binoculars on the ledge in front of the window and clasped his hands behind his back. He resisted the urge to smile, though he couldn't wait to surprise the two presidents once the weapons were airborne.

One of the guards tried to tell the command center something, but his words were broken up by static, likely caused by electronic interference.

"Did anyone understand what he was trying to say?" Sinclair asked.

One of the men seated at the controls offered an explanation. "I think he was asking what to do with the prisoner."

"Open the channel," Sinclair said. "Bring him to me so I can make an example out of him."

"Roger that," replied the guard.

"All right," Sinclair said as he rubbed his hands together. "It's show time."

Another man's voice boomed over the loudspeaker. "Launching the rockets in t-minus fifteen seconds, fourteen, thirteen, twelve . . ."

CHAPTER 21

HAWK RESISTED THE URGING of the two security guards until they started whacking him with night sticks. Upon relenting, he went without incident to the makeshift holding cell they had in the security office. They chained Hawk to an empty desk and dared him to move.

He scanned the room, searching for anything to help get out of the situation. He spotted a paperclip nearby on the floor and hatched a quick plan.

"I need to go to the restroom," Hawk said. "Can you help a guy out?"

The guard rolled his eyes. "Hold it."

"I can't. I'm sure you understand."

The guard grunted. "Of course I do. But when I can't go, I do like most adults do and hold it. Do you want me to get you a nappy?"

"You Aussies have such strange words. So, no. I don't want a diaper. I need to pee, and I'm not going to hold it any longer."

"For goodness sake, Marcus," the guard staring at a bank of security cameras across the room chimed, "take the man the loo. Just keep his hands chained together. It's not like he can go anywhere. Better to do it now than keep Sinclair waiting when he summons the prisoner."

"Fine," the guard mumbled. "Up you go."

He used a zip tie to secure Hawk's hands in front of him before removing the handcuffs. Then the guard nudged Hawk forward. Sticking with his plan, as soon as the guard made contact with Hawk, he stumbled and fell face first onto the floor. The guard growled and kicked Hawk in the side.

"Get up!" Hawk slowly stood but not before swiping the paperclip. He tucked it in his pocket before the man could see what he was doing.

When Hawk returned from the restroom, one of his wrists was placed in a cuff and tethered back to the desk. Waiting patiently for the guard to become interested in something else, Hawk got his opportunity and began picking the lock the moment the man looked away. The process took longer than usual since Hawk had to keep an eye out for anyone who might catch him in the act. But he loosened the latch before it flung open, springing him free.

However, he didn't make a run for it right away. He was at a huge disadvantage since both guards carried weapons and he didn't have anything.

"Is there any possibility that I could get a cup of water?" Hawk asked. "I'm really parched."

One of the guards rolled his eyes. "You're lucky the boss didn't let me shoot you on the spot. Because I would've gladly put you down, you miserable excuse for a human being."

Hawk resisted any pithy comeback lines. "Please? I'm very thirsty."

"Marcus, get the man something to drink," the other guard said with the wave of his hand. "You don't have to treat him like a caged animal. Sinclair will take care of that."

The man huffed as he stomped out of the room. He returned a half-minute later with a cup of water, but as soon as the man handed it to Hawk, he splashed it back in the man's face and kicked his kneecap, sending him sprawling to the floor. Before the man could regain his bearings, Hawk snatched the guard's gun and took two shots at the man sitting behind the controls. Seconds later, he slumped forward and smacked his head on the panels.

When Hawk looked down, he noticed the other guard squirming away. Hawk put his foot on the man's head and applied enough pressure to pin him to the floor.

"What's the fastest way out of here?" Hawk asked.

The man stuttered as he explained the quickest exit route. After he finished, Hawk shot the man then collected both access badges before shoving the bodies into a hallway closet.

After retrieving his rucksack, Hawk put his com unit back into his ear and tried to reach Alex.

"You out there, Alex?" he asked.

Nothing.

He pulled out the device and inspected it. The side was crushed, enough to let Hawk know the guards had fiddled with it somehow.

Hawk hustled outside, following the directions the guard had related. While Hawk wasn't completely positive the man had told the truth, if he was lying, he was convincing. But with nothing else to go on, Hawk chose to believe the man was being honest.

Hawk rushed down several corridors before he reached the main launch area. The moment he did, he heard a roar and looked up in time to see the rockets blasting skyward.

He shook his head and cursed. Apparently, his efforts had failed.

Without hesitating, he scaled the wall again and headed back to Alex and Mia. They needed to regroup and come up with another plan—if there was still time.

CHAPTER 22

ALEX WANTED TO CURL up in a ball and cry. Without knowing where Hawk was or what was happening to him, she knew she required some extra tenacity to stay on task and finish the job. In the meantime, she was taking orders from Mia on the necessary steps to gain access to the rockets' controls.

"I'm sorry about Hawk," Mia said.

"He's not dead. At least, not yet anyway," Alex said. "He's come back from far worse situations than this."

"I hope you're right," Mia said. "We might still need him. I wish we had a way to communicate with him now."

"That makes two of us. But it's obvious they destroyed his earpiece. However, if he ever makes it back here, I've got another one for him."

Mia stopped and glanced at Alex. "You brought a backup pair?"

"I've got two extras. I've been doing this long enough to know that anything can and will go wrong.

It's a common occurrence on every mission, no matter how many times I double and triple check our tech."

"Maybe you need a new manufacturer," Mia said. "I know a guy who can make top of the line stuff that's nearly indestructible."

"I'll have to keep that in mind," Alex said. "But that doesn't do us a lot of good right now."

"Right," Mia said, her keys flying across the keyboard. "We're almost there."

The two women worked in silence, scrambling to get a connection with the weapons. After a couple minutes, they heard the rockets soar overhead.

"Almost there," Mia said.

A few seconds later, she pumped her fist before slamming it on the table.

"You did it," Alex said. "We're in."

"See if you can access the navigational tools," Mia said.

Alex studied her screen before deciding what course of action to take. She identified a directory she thought would give her the power to redirect the weapons wherever she wanted. After a couple more minutes, she held her hand up to Mia for a high five.

"I'm driving this machine now," Alex said. "Where should we send it?"

"Do you have the coordinates for Falcon Sinclair's mansion?" Mia asked.

Alex chuckled. "Now that would be one for the revenge hall of fame."

"I'm only joking. I'd put it in the water so you could retrieve it and study what he's doing."

Alex shook her head. "These rockets aren't what we should be most afraid of."

Mia furrowed her brow. "What do you mean?"

"When we were on the plane, I started digging deeper into those files," Alex said. "And I realized there was more to the plan than just long-range missiles. Those things are a dime a dozen in today's high-tech world of illegal arms dealing. If you want to fire at someone who's a thousand miles away, you can find someone to sell you the mechanism to do that. It takes just a few clicks on the dark web and a boat load of cash, but you can have the weapon of your dreams."

"So, what did you find?"

"I uncovered a hidden file, an Easter egg that Tyler Timmons had nested inside the encrypted files. He only wanted the right people to find it, so he made a little map inside. See."

Alex pointed at her screen and showed Mia the fruit of Timmons's labor.

"How did I miss that?" Mia asked.

"When you're a hacker, you deal in code and see life through the lens of code. But sometimes you have to step back from what you're working on and consider the possibilities that there's more to see. While those rockets are destructive, I had a hunch there was more to what Sinclair was doing."

"What are you trying to say?"

"These rockets are merely a demonstration of the real star of the show—a satellite weapons defense system that can eliminate a threat before it even arrives."

Before Alex could continue her explanation, her laptop started beeping. She let out a few choice words and then stared slack-jawed at the screen.

"What is it?" Mia asked, crowding over Alex's shoulder.

"We lost our connection."

"How is that possible?" Mia asked as she nudged Alex aside and typed away on the keyboard.

"I don't know, but something disconnected us."

Alex sighed. "We need to find out what's going on in that control room."

"Already on it," Mia said, sliding back to her seat. "I don't have time to hack all the way into the mainframe, but I started cracking the ancillary functions like the intercom system and other things that aren't as well guarded."

"And?"

"I'm almost there. Give me another minute, and

we might be able to hear what's going on in that room with Sinclair."

While Alex was waiting for Mia to finish, both women were startled when they heard footsteps drawing nearer. Alex poked her head outside the tent and saw a shadowy figure closing in on their position. She darted back inside and grabbed her gun. When she emerged from the door, she had it trained straight ahead.

"Whoa, whoa, whoa!" Hawk said, his hands raised in the air. "It's me."

Alex dropped the weapon and sprinted toward him, clobbering him with a hug. "I wasn't sure we'd see you again."

"We're not safe yet," Hawk said. "Sinclair is going to have his minions combing the island as soon as the two bodies of those guards I killed are discovered. We need to get moving right now."

"Actually, we're not going anywhere," Alex said. "In fact, I'm sending you right back into the fire."

"Are you serious?" Hawk asked as he eyed her carefully.

"As a heart attack," Alex said.

"Good work on the transmitter," Mia said without looking up from her screen.

"I'm fortunate Sinclair's goons didn't shoot me on the spot," he said to Mia before turning to Alex. "Why do I need to go back?"

"The transmitter stopped working," Mia said without waiting for Alex to answer.

"What?" Hawk asked. "How?"

Alex shrugged. "I have no idea. We think maybe their onboard computer detected an intrusion and shut us down. But the bottom line is that we have no way of communicating with that rocket."

"Unless I go back?"

She nodded. "It's the only way. We need you to help us connect to the mainframe. We can't hack it from here without a direct connection. And the only way we're going to be able to redirect the missiles to a harmless landing is if we piggyback onto the command center computer and override the GPS system from there."

"Are you trying to get me killed?" Hawk asked.

Alex put her hands on Hawk's shoulders. "Honey, I love you, but the world needs you right now. We're still trying to figure out what Sinclair is doing in there, but I read on one of the dark web sites that President Karelin is supposedly meeting with Sinclair this week too."

"Sinclair has the American and Russian presidents together in the same room?" Hawk said. "That can't be good."

"And that's exactly why we need you to gain access to the mainframe for us. Think you can handle it?"

Hawk nodded. "Yeah, but not alone."

Mia threw her hands in the air and shouted. "Everyone, shut up. I've got the audio from the room with Sinclair and Young."

Mia turned up the volume and leaned back in her chair.

"Gentlemen, I brought you here today to experience the power of my company's new Force Field protection program," Sinclair said. "If you thought Ronald Reagan's vision for the so-called Star Wars program was revolutionary, today you'll get to witness the realization of that dream—and so much more. Whoever possesses this defense system will be solidified as a world superpower, they'll become *the* world superpower. No foreign entity will be able to touch you, while you'll be free to wreak havoc on any nation you so desire without any violent repercussions."

"This is why you brought us together?" Young asked.

Sinclair chuckled. "Did you think I brought you here to simply wine and dine you? There's only one system, and it's open to the highest bidder. But enough talk. Once those missiles reach orbit, I'm going to show you what this system is capable of."

"Understand now why this is so important?" Alex asked Hawk.

"I'm gonna need your help," he said.

She handed him a receiver. "Put this in. I'll be with you every step of the way. We don't have a second to waste."

"No, Alex, you're not understanding what I'm saying," he said. "I need you *with* me. We need to go do this together."

"And who's going to handle the logistics from here?" Alex asked.

"I think Mia is more than capable of handling everything on this end," he said. "I might be tempted to take her, but I know how proficient you are with a gun."

"Definitely rules me out," Mia said.

Hawk crammed the listening piece into his ear and handed the other one to Mia. "We need you to be communicating with us every step of the way."

Alex grabbed her backpack. "Mia, you can do this."

Mia nodded. "You patch me into that mainframe, and I'll do my best to stop this catastrophe from happening."

Hawk tightened his rucksack and looked at Alex.

"Are you ready?" he asked.

"Is anyone ever ready for something like this?"

"Not really," Hawk said. "It's time to move."

They exited the tent in a full sprint back toward

the facility. This time, Hawk's lungs burned more than ever before, the burden heavier than ever before.

"We can do this, Hawk," Alex said, her voice ringing loud and clear through his listening piece.

"I know I'm capable," Hawk said. "But I don't think you understand just how dangerous Sinclair is."

"If I didn't before, I do now."

"So where is this mainframe located?" Hawk asked.

There was a long pause.

"Alex?"

"Yeah."

"Did you hear my question?" he asked.

"Yep," she said, stopping for a moment to catch her breath.

Hawk slowed down when he realized she wasn't with him. He turned back, jogging toward her.

"Well, are you going to answer me then?"

She looked down at the forest floor. "It's ten stories below the surface."

Hawk didn't react. "Let's go then. We don't have a second to lose."

CHAPTER 23

Washington, D.C.

BAS HAWK AND ALEX NEARED the compound, they found a half-dozen guards combing the forest for the escaped prisoner. He gestured toward a fallen log, and then the two of them took cover beneath it.

"That didn't take long," Alex whispered.

"We can't get caught, but we can't let them stray too far from here or else they're going to find Mia."

"What's the plan?"

"Just stay close and get ready to run," Hawk said.

He grabbed a grenade from his rucksack and pulled the pin. With a giant heave, he tossed the explosive device over a hill in the opposite direction of Mia and the tent. The explosion sent the guards diving to the ground before they got up and raced in the direction of the grenade. Hawk and Alex remained low until all of the guards had streamed by in search of the perpetrator.

"Let's go," Hawk said.

They stayed low as they hustled from tree to tree, avoiding detection. Nodding at the man inside the guard house, Hawk kept his gun low. When the man protested, Hawk fired one shot into the man's chest. Alex took the access card Hawk had swiped off one of the men he'd killed earlier and released the lock on the gate. Hawk grabbed the man's walkie-talkie in order to keep tabs on the men in pursuit.

"We're inside, Mia," Hawk said. "But there are guards combing the area. Just watch your six."

"My what?" she asked.

"Watch your back," Alex said. "I left a gun for you underneath the chair. Now might be a good time to pull it out just in case someone gives you any trouble."

"I don't know how to use a gun," Mia said.

"Just point and shoot—and then run," Alex said.

Hawk scanned his card and then rushed into the building with Alex right behind him. They hustled down the hallway until they reached the elevators. Once inside, Hawk searched for the button to take them to the server room ten floors below ground.

"Where's the button for the basement?" he asked, staring at the panel.

"There's not one," Alex said. "You need a key."

Hawk let out a string of expletives and slammed his hand against the elevator wall.

"Maybe I can help," Mia said. "Just give me a second."

"I'm not sure we even have that much time," Hawk said. "Those rockets will target something very soon."

"Working as fast as I can," she said.

As Hawk paced around waiting for Mia to figure out a way to get the elevator to descend to the bowels of the Obsidian facility, the doors slid open. He and Alex darted inside, pressing their backs flat against the side. Moments later, two guards entered.

Hawk and Alex acted immediately to gain the upper hand. Catching both men by surprise, Hawk delivered a throat punch to the man closest to him. Alex delivered a hearty kick right between the legs of the man nearest to her, stunning him and sending him to the ground in pain. Hawk put both men down, two shots each, one center mass and the other in the head. Hawk hit the button that closed the doors and stepped back over the bodies.

"Okay," Mia said, "is everything all right? I thought I heard some tussling in the background."

"We're fine, Mia," Hawk said between clenched teeth. "Wanna get us outta here?"

"I thought you'd never ask," she said.

Hawk and Alex stumbled as the elevator began a rapid descent ten floors below the surface. Using his foot, Hawk shoved aside one of the bodies of the men whose head kept bumping into him.

"Making you uncomfortable?" Alex asked as she cast a furtive glance at the body near Hawk's feet.

He chuckled. "I'm not nearly as uncomfortable as that guy is right now."

Alex wasn't amused. "Let's stay alert. We're far from being out of the woods just yet."

When the doors opened, Hawk and Alex stayed back, unsure if the men down there were aware of what was happening up on the surface. And based on the surroundings, Hawk wasn't sure they would have a clue.

Hawk and Alex slid the bodies against the wall so they wouldn't be visible when the doors parted. And seconds after they did, Hawk didn't hear anything, just a low humming permeating throughout a vast room.

At ten floors below the surface, the space wasn't just for keeping servers in a cool spot. The ceiling was ten meters high, comprising a space of about a hundred meters by fifty meters and housing long missiles and other weapons.

"What is this place?" Alex asked.

Hawk shook his head. "I don't know. Whatever it is, it's not good. But we can't worry about that right now. We need to find that server room. Are you sure it's down here?"

She nodded. "Mia?"

"I'm here."

"Do you have the schematics up of this building?"

"I'm staring at them right now," Mia said.

"Can you direct us to the server room from the elevators?"

"I'll do my best."

Mia started giving directions, but a bullet whistling past Hawk's head cut them short. He dove to the floor behind some crates, yanking Alex down with him.

"We can't get in a long gunfight," she said.

"I know," Hawk said before he popped up and fired a shot toward the hostiles.

"By my best estimation, we've got about five minutes before those missiles are redirected toward some highly populated place."

"What makes you think Sinclair isn't doing anything other than a demonstration?"

"He doesn't like to waste time or money. And a demonstration would be throwing away both."

Hawk nodded. "Guess I better clear a path for us."

He didn't hesitate, rising and putting two shots in the man firing at them. As another guard rushed in to help, Hawk gunned him down too with a pair of bullets to the chest.

Hawk waited a moment and didn't hear any movement. "I think we got them. Let's move."

They stayed low, hustling in the direction Mia had told them the server room was located. When they reached it, Hawk realized facial recognition was required to enter. He sprinted back to one of the guard's bodies and dragged it over. Using the man's key card, Hawk swiped it before propping the man's head up in front of the access camera. The light at the bottom of the panel turned green, followed by a mechanical click.

Alex grabbed the handle and pulled down.

"Looks like we're in," she said as she put her shoulder into the door and pushed forward.

"All right," Hawk said. "Mia, you're up. What do we do next?"

"What does the room look like?" Mia asked.

Hawk's eyes widened as he surveyed the area. "It just looks like rows and rows of bookshelves covered with computers to me."

"Alex?"

Alex chuckled. "I doubt Hawk's ever seen a computer room like this before. I'll take over."

"You need to find the terminal," Mia said. "This isn't a server farm. The mainframe is one giant computer."

"So are we looking for a keyboard and a monitor?" Hawk asked as he hustled around the room.

"Yes, that will be the entry point to the system," Mia said. "If you can patch me in there, I'll be able to wreak havoc on their system."

"I'm on it," Alex said. "Hawk, you just watch the door."

A shattering sound interrupted Hawk's train of thought. The lone looking window glass splintered, leaving them more exposed than ever. He dove and instructed Alex to do the same. Shards of glass pricked his hands as he army crawled to the back wall and took up a position behind a server unit.

"Hawk!" Alex cried. "I've been hit."

He sprang from his spot and darted over to Alex, who hadn't moved. Her left arm was gushing with blood. Hawk ripped off the bottom part of his shirt and formed a makeshift tourniquet for her.

"You're gonna be all right," he said. "It looks like the bullet went all the way through."

She gritted her teeth. "We've gotta finish this thing. If Sinclair directs those missiles at a city—"

"I'm on it," he said as he handed her another gun and took the transmitter device from her. "Just in case you need extra protection."

Alex winced in pain and slid to the floor, clutching her arm with her left hand while holding the weapon in her right.

"Mia, what do I need to do?" Hawk asked.

"Just put that transmitter near the terminal, and I should be able to hack it."

"Roger that."

Two more shots ripped through the room housing the mainframe.

"Hawk!" Alex cried. "They're coming. Hurry."

He found the terminal and placed the transmitter underneath the keyboard tray. "Okay, Mia. You should be good to go now."

After another shot ripped through the room, Hawk hustled back toward Alex. She grimaced as she glanced at her wound.

"You're gonna be all right, honey," Hawk said as he took the gun from her.

More bullets whizzed past them, peppering the wall.

"Mia, you don't have much time," Hawk said. "We're getting pinned down here."

CHAPTER 24

FALCON SINCLAIR TEMPLED his fingers as he paced in front of the world's most powerful presidents. He wore a satisfied grin as he prepared to give the speech he'd rehearsed so many times before. With one quick sideways glance at his captive audience, he took a deep breath and launched into his speech.

"Gentlemen," he said, stopping and turning to face them, "now that I have your attention and the missiles are off, we need to talk about the real reason you're here today."

President Young scowled. "You told me you wanted to show me a weapon you'd invented."

Sinclair laughed and shook his head. "So gullible, just like the American people. If they weren't such fools, you'd never be in this position. But here you are, a career politician, standing tall after walking on the backs of everyday citizens."

Young bristled at the characterization of his rise

to power. "If you wanted this to be a referendum on my ability to govern, you could've just lodged a complaint on the White House website."

Sinclair chuckled again, this time joined by President Karelin. "You think this is about you? I'm afraid you've misread my statement. No, the reason we're here today is to discuss the new global era we're about to enter into. You see, in the past, the world has been ruled by powerful nations. And people such as yourselves have been seated upon thrones, real or virtual, that have allowed you to operate wherever you please with complete autonomy and zero accountability. Well, that ends today. Moving forward, I will be the one ruling the world, and one of you will do my bidding."

"One of us?" Karelin asked.

Sinclair grinned and rubbed his hands together. "That's right. You're both here because in order to have an auction, you need at least two people."

Young scowled. "An auction? For what?"

"I'm glad you asked, *Mr. President*. For a long time, it's been the dream of both your countries to develop a satellite weapons defense system that would prevent any airborne attack. Well, gentlemen, welcome to the future."

Sinclair turned and gestured toward the bank of screens on the far wall. Placing his hands behind his back, he strode toward the wall and continued.

"The Castle-74 is the culmination of years of work by many of my dedicated staffers from various companies I oversee. We pride ourselves on developing solutions for the real world as well as inspiring imaginations. A long time ago, my imagination was inspired to become the most powerful man on the planet. And since I wasn't interested in playing the political game, I forged a different path, one that has led me to a final destination with an audience of the two of you. What plays out over the next few minutes will determine the course of history as well as the conduit through which I shall govern the world."

Karelin cocked his head to one side and furrowed his brow. "I'm not sure I understand."

"Let me explain," Sinclair said. "The two of you preside over massive budgets, compiled from money that you've extracted from hard-working citizens one way or another. But instead of building a better world, you've hoarded your wealth, investing it in all the wrong things. For example, there's no excuse that either one of your two countries haven't invented a cure for cancer or created a better health care system that doesn't leave someone broke or either dead in the waiting room. Meanwhile, you both stoke the fires of war, banging the drums for political gain. That must end now."

"Why?" Young asked. "So we yield our power to you? I don't think so."

Sinclair smirked. "It's happening one way or another, Mr. Young, whether you like it or not. The only real question is if you're going to be my partner in all this or my foe. And I can assure you that you don't want to be my foe."

"This is absurd," Young said. "I'm leaving."

"You might want to wait a minute or two before you storm out of here," Sinclair said as he produced two small pads and a pair of pens from his jacket pocket. "We're about to have a fun exercise, and if you don't participate, I can promise you'll have no home to go back to."

Karelin snatched the materials from Sinclair, while Young turned back toward the billionaire and took the items begrudgingly.

"Now, I want you to make a short list," Sinclair said. "Write down the name of three cities you'd like to see obliterated, preferably in the country of your enemy here."

"I'm not doing this," Young said.

But before he could finish his sentence, Karelin hurriedly jotted down a few things on his paper.

"It's up to you," Sinclair said, "but I can promise you'll completely regret it if you don't."

DIVIDE AND CONQUER | 209

Young sighed, unsure if he was playing right into Sinclair's hands through this exercise. Then Young pondered if Sinclair genuinely had the type of weapon to wipe out an entire city—or if he'd really do it. Instead of balking at the request again, Young joined in, scribbling down the names of several Russian cities.

After a minute, Sinclair declared that time was up and snatched the pieces of paper from the presidents' hands. "Are we ready to begin?"

Sinclair didn't wait for an answer as he focused his attention on the screens behind him. A simulation of a rocket launch appeared on the screen, showing the missiles soaring over the earth.

"Now I'm going to put on a demonstration for you," Sinclair said. "However, only one of you will have a city protected by Castle-74, while the other of you will have to scramble jets to the sky. And such efforts will be woefully late."

"This is ridiculous," Young said.

"Characterize it however you wish, but the reality you're dealing with is that one of the cities on President Karelin's list of places he'd like to obliterate in the United States is going to have a missile aimed at it. And one of the Russian cities you wrote down will also have a missile pointed at it. But there's just one problem. The Castle-74 can only protect one country. And that's going to be the highest bidder. Let's start the bidding at five hundred billion. Seems reasonable, yes?"

"I'm not buying this," Young said. "You wouldn't dare attempt something like that."

"Believe what you may, but understand that this is very serious," Sinclair said. "And if you aren't interested in playing along, you're going to have a mess to clean up when you return to Washington, at least what's left of it."

"While we might be enemies ideologically, neither I nor President Karelin would be interested in this twisted game of yours," Young said.

"Are you sure about that?" Sinclair asked.

Karelin stroked his chin as his gaze bounced between Sinclair and Young. "Five hundred billion."

"Excellent," Sinclair said. "Still uninterested, President Young?"

Young clenched his jaw and glared at Karelin. "Six hundred billion."

A faint smile spread across Sinclair's lips. "Do I hear seven hundred billion?"

CHAPTER 25

HAWK RELOADED AND RETURNED fire on the guards outside. But almost as soon as the gunfight started, it abruptly halted. A man rushed onto the scene and scolded the men for firing so close to the computer.

"Come on, Alex," Hawk said. "We need to take cover on the other side of this machine."

He helped her to her feet and covered her as they eased around the mainframe.

"Mia," Hawk said into his coms, "how's it looking?"

"I've almost breached the firewall," Mia said.

"Make it quick. We're about to have company, and I don't know what that's going to mean for your access."

"Is the transmitter visible?" she asked.

"It's on the keyboard tray."

"Hide it now," Mia said.

Hawk didn't hesitate, darting over to the terminal and tucking the wireless transmitter out of sight.

"Done," he announced as he slid next to Alex.

"Great," Mia said, her keyboard clicking in the background. "And I'm in."

Alex pumped her left fist before she stopped and winced in pain.

"Just take it easy," Hawk said.

"I'm trying," she said.

"Look, we're going to get out of this."

She leaned her head against the wall and looked upward. "How can you be so sure? We're kind of hemmed in at the moment, and there's nobody else on this godforsaken island who can help us."

"We'll figure out a way. You've got to trust me on this one, but please be careful with that arm of yours."

Alex examined the weapon in her right hand. "At least I can still shoot."

He dug another gun out of his rucksack and gave it to her. "You've got eight shots on that one in case you run out. Choose your targets wisely."

"I always do," she said with a wry grin. "You know how much I hate wasting bullets."

"At least you still have your sense of humor."

Mia interrupted the moment, squawking on the coms. "I'm in. I'm in."

"Do you have control yet?" Alex asked.

"Working on it," Mia said. "Give me another minute or two."

The door was positioned on the far side of the room around several rows of servers. Hawk crept around the side to see if there was any activity taking place outside. Using a bank of computers for cover, he could see the entrance. And while he couldn't make out what the men were saying, he could hear them speaking in hushed tones.

Hawk grabbed the walkie-talkie he'd lifted off the guard at the gate and turned up the volume to listen in on their conversation.

"We're down here with the mainframe," one of the men said. "We've got at least two hostiles pinned down. I think one of them is injured."

"How many men are with you?"

"Four."

"Sit tight, and I'll send some more. Don't take any action until you have reinforcements. The intruder is well-trained and should be considered extremely dangerous."

"Copy that," the man responded.

Hawk rushed back over to Alex. "We're about to be heavily outnumbered."

"What's that mean?" she asked.

"I think it means we're done here."

Alex clenched her jaw and shook her head subtly. "They're gonna kill us, aren't they?"

Hawk nodded. "Probably. But that doesn't mean

I'm going to just lie down and take it."

"Do you have a plan?"

"It's an idea at this point, but it's about the only one I can think of."

"Will it work?"

He shrugged. "It all depends."

"On what?"

"Lady Luck."

"Well, let's just do what we can until Mia makes a connection with the rockets," she said.

Mia let out a yelp that pierced Hawk's ear.

"Please don't yell like that again," he said.

"I'm in the program controlling the missiles," Mia said. "I'm going to lock in a course for them to land harmlessly in the water."

"Good work, Mia," Alex said. "I knew bringing you along was the best thing we could've done."

"How are things looking for you two?" Mia asked.

"Not so good. Just remember what I told you about hiding and the flare gun in case we don't come back," Hawk said.

"Wait. What? You might not make it out of there?"

"Just focus, Mia," Alex said. "Don't worry about all that. We'll figure out something. Just keep doing what you're doing."

Alex cocked her head to one side and glared at

Hawk as she muted her microphone. "Couldn't you have just lied there? She's not trained like us. If she isn't fully concentrating, we could be in big trouble."

"She needed to know the truth for her own sake," Hawk said. "Her survival might depend on it."

"You should've at least waited."

"We may not have an opportunity to say anything once those guards storm through the door. Better to give her a fighting chance than leave her in the dark."

Hawk and Alex sat in silence for a minute, waiting for movement from either the guards outside or a report from Mia as to which course of action to take next.

"You know what the worst part of this is?" Alex asked, breaking the silence.

Hawk chuckled. "We may never get to watch a Bollywood movie together again?"

She exhaled slowly. "That would be disappointing. But, no, the worst part is that we might die only trying to delay the inevitable. Once we're gone, there might not be anyone standing in opposition to someone like Falcon Sinclair. He'll just pick up where he left off moments after his guards feed our bodies to the sharks."

"But we have to try," Hawk said. "If we don't fight, we might as well roll out the red carpet for the sonofabitch. Edmund Burke once said, 'When bad men combine, the good must associate; else they will fall, one by one, an unpitied sacrifice in a contemptible struggle.' I know what I signed up for when I started this job, and I'll be damned if my death is going to be an unpitied sacrifice."

"You really think there's enough good men in this world to prevail over evil like Sinclair?"

"I have hope that there is, but if we don't fight, we'll never know. But now's not the time for philosophical reflection. We're not dead yet."

"Guys," Mia said over the coms.

"What is it, Mia?" Hawk asked.

Alex unmuted her mic. "What's going on?"

"This software has some incredible AI defense mechanisms that I've never encountered before. It's like the computer has a mind of its own and is fighting me to retake control."

"What are you saying?" Hawk asked.

"I'm saying I don't know how much longer I can maintain control."

"Can you lock in those coordinates so it can't be overridden?" Alex asked.

"I can try."

Before the conversation could continue, the door flew open and several guards poured inside. They descended upon Hawk and Alex with weapons trained. Hawk gave Alex a knowing look, and she lowered her gun. They placed their pistols on the floor and raised their hands.

"Where is it?" the head guard asked as he strode up to his captives.

"Where's what?" Hawk asked.

The man clasped his hands behind his back and glared at Hawk. "You know what I'm talking about. The wireless transmitter that's enabling you to control our rockets."

"Why don't you search the room yourself?" Hawk suggested. "Or I'll tell you myself if you allow us to walk out of here."

The man nodded at one of the guards, who rushed over to Alex and jammed the nozzle of his gun into her head.

"That's not necessary," Hawk said.

"I'm afraid it is, Mr. Hawk, given your penchant for uncooperative behavior. You're going to tell me where the transmitter is. And you're going to tell me right now."

CHAPTER 26

YOUNG EYED THE RUSSIAN president, who didn't seem fazed by the auction. While Young couldn't allow one of his own cities to be decimated, he wondered how much longer Sinclair would continue pitting the two leaders against each other. Sinclair was already a billionaire, and one of the richest in the world at that. Young wondered if the end game was to be the world's first trillionaire and use his money to indulge himself. But despite Sinclair's giant ego, Young figured there had to be some other motivation than greed.

"Do I hear two point one trillion?" Sinclair asked as he turned his gaze toward Young.

Young sighed and shook his head. "I think I've reached my limit. I can't participate in this farce any longer."

"Oh, Mr. President, I can assure you that I'm very serious about carrying through with my promise," Sinclair said. "If I never followed through with my threats, I would've never reached the heights that I have with my business. Now, perhaps you want reconsider withdrawing from the bidding, no?"

"There comes a point when a man must stand up to extortion," Young said.

"And apparently, that point for you is at two trillion dollars."

"I don't believe you'll do it."

"So, you're testing me?"

Young nodded. "I'm calling your bluff. If you dared to launch an attack on Washington, you'd be signing your death warrant."

"That's hardly the case," Sinclair said. "You'd have to invade a sovereign nation to get me. And I'm counting on President Karelin being satisfied with our product. So much so that he'd protect me."

"Your suppositions may be the death of you."

"Or it may be what I need to rise to power."

"I'm walking out of here," Young said, "and there's nothing you can do to stop me."

"I beg to differ," Sinclair said as he nodded at one of his guards standing near the door. The man slid in front of Young, impeding his exit.

"If that door isn't open where I can walk through it in five seconds, I'm going to call for my Secret Service detail. And I promise you'll regret it."

"I doubt that," Sinclair said. He turned toward the

screen as it switched from the simulated missile trajectory to the cameras outside the control center. The security details for both the American and Russian presidents were lying on their backs, apparently out from some type of gas.

"What's this?" Karelin asked.

"I needed assurance that neither of you would walk out and risk this event that my team has been planning for months," Sinclair said. "I really hate delays."

"I demand that you stop this at once," Karelin said.

"Oh, so you don't want the winning bid? I can direct both missiles toward your countries and keep you sequestered here while your subordinates get access to nuclear codes and launch warheads back and forth at one another. Is that what you want?"

"Of course not," Karelin said.

Sinclair turned toward Young. "And you, Mr. President?"

"I'll stay."

"Excellent," Sinclair said. "Now that we have that all cleared up, shall we continue?"

He marched over to the control panel on the wall and returned to the screen containing the simulated images of the two missiles streaking across the planet.

"Now, I'm not a fool," Sinclair said. "And it might

be unwise for me to simply demand money, especially an amount as enormous as two trillion dollars. I'm quite certain neither one of you would like to see that amount vanish from your country's treasury, would you?"

Both men shook their head.

"In that case, let me make you another offer," Sinclair said as he paced around the room. "Instead of pitting you against each other and starting a world war, I am amenable to a different type of arrangement, contingent upon the fact that you both agree to it."

Karelin stroked his beard. "I'm listening."

"I would like a place on your senior level cabinet, a guaranteed spot among the men you count as your trusted advisors. But it would be a secret position, one that would protect us from being impugned by the reckless press corps."

Young waited, pausing to see if Karelin would speak first—and he did.

"I would prefer just to hand you the money," Karelin said. "The defense system, if it's as good as you say it is, is worth money. However, I would like to see it in action first."

Young nodded and lied. "Perhaps we could come to agreement as well. But like my good comrade here, I'm not agreeing to anything until I see how it works."

"In that case, let's start with the man who made the winning bid, shall we?" Sinclair said.

Sinclair strode over to a computer terminal and typed on the keyboard. When he was finished, he looked up and smiled.

"You're about to see the new course for the missiles appear on the screen," he said.

As soon as he finished speaking, a new simulated image materialized, showing that one of the missiles was headed straight for Washington.

"All I have to do to make that happen is press this button," Sinclair said. "Is everyone ready?"

Before he even finished asking the question, he pressed the button, initiating the strike sequence.

He grinned as he studied the picture on the screen in front of him. "T-minus ninety seconds and counting. Are you ready to be amazed?"

CHAPTER 27

HAWK STOOD, KEEPING his hands raised in the air. He moved slowly toward the mainframe and opened the door. Once the keyboard and terminal were exposed, he gestured toward them.

"If you'll notice right here underneath the keyboard tray, you'll see the transmitter," Hawk said.

The commander nodded at one of the guards, who walked over to the terminal and inspected the machine. As he did, all eyes focused on his movements, giving Hawk the opportunity he needed to flip the room.

Hawk turned his body to the side so that his raised right hand remained visible but his left hand yanked a grenade off his belt.

"I got it," the guard yelled. "How do I turn it off?"

"There's a switch on the back that will allow you to cease all communications with any other devices," Alex offered.

He flipped it over and followed Alex's instructions.

"What just happened?" Mia asked over the coms.

Hawk and Alex remained quiet.

"Don't leave me in the dark here, guys," Mia said. "Somebody tell me what's going on in there. I just lost my connection right as I entered in the new coordinates. I have no idea who's in control of the missiles now."

As Alex was talking, Hawk pulled out the pin of the grenade and held the explosive device tight. In the commotion, the guards took their eyes off him just long enough for him to attempt to regain the upper hand.

The mainframe was centered against the far wall. Aside from the small clearing directly around the computer, the rest of the room was filled with rows of servers, stacked one right on top of the other, floor to ceiling. However, a gap in the middle of each row provided an escape route for him and Alex. But that was all contingent upon his ability to create an opportunity to use it.

"You guys need to act now," Mia said over the coms. "I just searched the coordinates that I captured earlier. Sinclair is aiming those missiles straight at Washington."

Hawk didn't move, wondering how long it would take before any of the guards realized he was holding a grenade.

One handed over the transmitter to his commander, who promptly dropped it on the floor and crushed it with his heel.

"Any questions?" the man asked.

One of the guards pointed at Hawk. "Why is this bloke holding a grenade?"

The commander glanced back at Hawk and growled. "What do you think you're doing?"

"Everyone, put your weapons down or we all die," Hawk said.

Unmoved by Hawk's threat, the commander just stared at him. "You're going to kill yourself, too?"

"We're just going to walk out of here," Hawk said, helping Alex to her feet before kneeling down and picking up his rucksack.

"I don't think so," the commander said, his gun trained on Hawk.

"Just ask yourself this question: Is the work you're doing for Falcon Sinclair worth dying for?"

Hawk tossed the grenade at the commander and then shoved Alex forward down the aisle. He darted a few meters before pulling her to the ground, utilizing the server units as cover.

The explosion rocked the room, leaving his ears ringing. He scrambled to his feet before retrieving another grenade from his pack. He pulled the pin out of the explosive device and slid it under the mainframe.

"Move," Hawk said to Alex.

They sprinted toward the door. As they reached the exit, the second blast rattled the room again, this time sparking a fire. The remaining glass shards still clinging to the window frame broke loose and shattered on the floor. All Hawk could hear were moans coming from the men as well as a buzzing fire alarm. Alex stopped and stared at the scene.

"Come on," Hawk said, tugging on her arm.

"Did you destroy the mainframe?" she asked.

"I hope so," Hawk said. "But I'm not going to sift through the ashes to find out. This area will be crawling with Sinclair's men any minute now if we don't get the hell outta here."

Alex nodded and took off running with Hawk.

A bullet whistled past, making Hawk rethink his exit strategy. He dashed to the right and hid behind a stack of wooden crates. When he peeked around the corner, he noticed two guards straggling forward with their guns trained.

Two more shots were fired, ricocheting off the wall behind them.

"Think you can still shoot?" Hawk asked.

Alex didn't hesitate to respond. "Give me a gun now."

They hunkered and prepared for another fight, one Hawk knew couldn't last long if they intended to escape the facility alive.

"Mia," Alex said over the coms.

"I'm here."

"Did we destroy the mainframe's ability to control the missiles?"

"I've got no idea," she said. "I'm in the dark right now, and there's not much more I can do other than try to listen in on Sinclair's meeting with the presidents."

Hawk checked his supply of munitions once more before reloading.

"Actually," he said, "there is one more thing you can do for us."

A machine gun blurted rounds at Hawk and Alex, sending them diving to the floor. Help had already arrived for Sinclair's men, and time was getting scarce.

CHAPTER 28

SINCLAIR PACED AROUND the room with his chest out and chin up. His crowning moment, the one he'd been working so hard to create for the past decade, was now upon him. With a memorable demonstration, he would show the leaders of the two most powerful nations in the world what he was capable of: utter chaos.

By pitting the two leaders against one another, Sinclair aimed to sow fear in the men. But his endgame wasn't about that at all. What he wanted was control and influence, the kind that can't be bought through bribes or votes. He—and he alone—would set the direction for the world by influencing both nations and ensuring their interests aligned with his. And most importantly, he'd answer to no one. Not a board who could fire him. Not an electorate who could choose someone else. Not a government that could forcibly remove him from power. No, Sinclair was going rule the world, and almost everyone on the planet would have no idea of his influence.

The simulation images on the monitors behind him continued to display the missiles heading for Washington, D.C. While he intended to demonstrate the power of the weapon's defense system, he could tell something was wrong when he tried to place the missiles' cameras up on the screen. In a flash, the televisions went dark.

"What is it now?" Sinclair grumbled. "Surely we're not going to miss this incredible moment."

A knock at the door arrested his attention.

"If you'll excuse me, gentlemen, I apparently need to attend to this," Sinclair said as he scurried across the room.

He checked the security cam to make sure one of his men stood outside before opening the door.

"What's this all about?" Sinclair asked in a hushed tone between clenched teeth.

"Sir, there's been an explosion downstairs in the computer room," the man explained.

"An explosion? A natural one or man-made?"

"We caught an American operative trespassing earlier on the premises. He somehow escaped and returned, this time with his intentions quite clear."

Sinclair scowled. "And what was that?"

"To destroy the mainframe."

"Did he succeed?"

"We're still trying to sort that out, sir. However, our ability to communicate with the missiles has been lost."

"What does that mean?"

"They're kind of on their own trajectory."

"Where are they headed?" Sinclair asked.

"Since the communication isn't working, we can't tell right now, but it's clear that a new heading was set by someone. And we can't do anything to stop it."

Sinclair shrugged. "We can still just shoot it down then, right?"

The man sighed. "That's the other thing, sir. The mainframe is also what we used to control the satellite weapons defense system."

"So, what you're saying is that we have missiles heading who knows where without any way of stopping it. Is that correct?"

The man nodded. "I'm afraid so, sir."

"Well, get the mainframe back online and get this situation fixed."

"But, sir, it's not that easy," the man said.

Sinclair set his jaw. "Do it."

He walked back into the room, eyeing his two guests.

"Is everything all right?" Karelin asked.

"Gentlemen, there's been a change of plans," Sinclair said.

"We can leave now?" Young asked. "Because I've had enough of this charade."

Sinclair shook his head. "I'm going to postpone the demonstration of the satellite weapons defense system until we can resolve some technical glitches."

"We're just supposed to sit around and wait for you and your team to get your act together?" Young asked. "With a defense system this reliable, I doubt it'd be worth having."

"Do you know what *unforeseen* means?" Sinclair asked.

Young sighed. "That's what happens in war. Your enemies do something unexpected, and if you can't adapt immediately, you're going to end up dead or captured. The fact that you've been in business as long as you have and don't understand this is appalling."

"Maybe I should just let those missiles strike Washington then?" Sinclair asked.

"From the way things sound, I don't think you could stop it now anyway," Young said. "And God help you if they do. You'll be hiding out in a cave, living off bugs, while the special forces units hunt you down to kill you."

Sinclair chuckled. "I doubt that. You have no idea what kind of power I have."

"Obviously not enough to run a routine demonstration of your innovative piece of technology."

"I have my fingers in every branch of your government."

Young shrugged. "Apparently it's not enough to get what you want. And I can promise you that no matter what you do, you're not going to get it."

Sinclair glared at Young. "That settles it. I'm going to let those missiles strike Washington. It'll make people forget the terrorist attacks on 9/11 ever happened. And all this will happen under your watch. That's how the American people will remember you."

"You're insane," Young said. "That will spark a world war." He turned toward Karelin. "Is that what you want?"

Karelin stroked his beard and looked wistfully off in the distance for a moment.

"Really? You want to go to war with us?" Young asked.

"If victory was assured, perhaps," Karelin said.

Sinclair grinned and put his arm around the Russian president. "This is a man who has what it takes to rule the world." Then the Australian glanced at Young. "You Americans have always been so weak."

"That's where you're wrong. Our restraint as a country is our strength."

"Restraint?" Sinclair said before snickering. "You are a bully who constantly sticks your nose in other people's fights only when it suits your own interest.

And only when you know you have the power to dictate the outcome you desire. You're like a wealthy parent using your money to manipulate your children."

"If that's how you view my great country, you lack an incredible amount of context regarding how we get involved in conflicts around the world. It's easy to claim the moral high ground when you live in an isolated place. Islands are great for hiding and indulging yourself, but our strength is forged in relationships that not only benefit us but also benefit the world."

Sinclair sneered. "I'm about to show you what real power is, the kind that can reshape the history of the world."

"And for what? A mention in the history books? You'll be dead within a week."

Sinclair pulled out his gun. "Or maybe you will, found on my yacht in your room with a self-inflicted gunshot wound to the head. You'll take the cowardly way out just like your predecessor."

"He didn't—" Young paused. "If your end game is to gain a position of influence within the U.S. government, you're not going to accomplish that by killing me, and you know it."

"Do I?" Sinclair asked. "Ask yourself, 'Why am I here right now? How did Falcon Sinclair arrange such a meeting?' When you consider the answer to those questions truthfully, it'll become clear just how much influence I have even within the White House."

"You're rich," Young said. "Money can buy you access but not always influence."

"My reach is greater than you think. My money bought your wife."

Young's nostrils flared, his eyes narrowing. "She's dead, you imbecile."

Sinclair cocked his head to one side. "Really? Are you sure about that? Have you seen her dead body?"

"I watched people scrape her charred remains up off my bedroom floor," Young said. "What kind of sadistic person are you to ask me such a question?"

"Sadistic? No. Sly as a fox? Most definitely. But rest assured, Mr. President, your wife is safe and sound under my care."

"What the hell are you talking about? Aren't you listening to me? Weren't you at her funeral?"

"I was at a memorial service, but I never saw a body."

"That's because there wasn't one."

Sinclair pointed his index finger at Young. "You're right about that. Because she was by a pool somewhere, safe and sound on the day you thought you buried her."

"That's bullshit, and you know it," Young said. "You might be able to manipulate most people, but I'm not falling for your games."

"This isn't a game, Mr. President. Would you like to see her again?"

Young pursed his lips and clenched his fists. He took a couple steps back before making a run at Sinclair with a wild swing. Sinclair slid aside and pushed Young, sending him sprawling to the ground.

"You were right earlier," Sinclair said as he walked over to Young as he slowly got up. "I've been in business long enough to understand that there are moments when something unexpected happens. And earlier, my mainframe getting sabotaged was one of those. However, I was ready for how to proceed, always equipped with a solid backup plan. But right now, you're the one who didn't see this coming. Your guards are all incapacitated, a missile is headed toward your country's capitol city, and you just found out that your wife conspired against you and isn't really dead. The pressing question is how are *you* going to handle these unforeseen events? Because right now, *mate*, it's you against the world."

Young stood before making another lunge at Sinclair, but he grabbed the American president's arms and flung him back down to the ground.

Sinclair paced around Young while Karelin took in the scene from the corner.

"Now," Sinclair said, "you can continue to attempt to solve this with physical violence, which I can assure you won't end well for you. Or you can walk out of here a free man and retain your power and position as the leader of one of the largest countries on Earth."

"What's the catch?" Young asked.

"There is no catch, as it were. There's simply the agreement that you will discuss all major decisions with me moving forward and heed my advice, even if it contradicts what your other advisors say. If not, I will unleash some of my weapons upon you—and you'll be powerless to stop them. Meanwhile, your war hawks will urge you to strike back at the Russians, but any such attempt will be swatted down by my defense system they own. Do you comprehend what I'm saying here?"

"I'd never agree to anything of the sort," Young said. "That's treason and would cause me to break the oath I pledged to fulfill in front of the American people."

Sinclair turned toward the screen and clicked the remote. An image of Madeline Young appeared. She was clad in a bathing suit and straw hat, relaxing poolside.

"Would you like to see her again?" Sinclair asked. "Would you like to live?"

"That's not her," Young said with a growl. "This ploy won't work on me."

"Oh, it's very much her. She's even reading her

favorite author right now, Jodi Picoult. If you'd like, I can even get her to speak."

"That's a recording. I'm not stupid."

"If it's not a live video, could I get the person filming it to do this?" Sinclair asked before he pulled out his phone and texted a message. Seconds later, the man capturing the footage placed a newspaper up in front of the camera, showing the day's date.

"Neat trick," Young said. "I'm still not falling for it."

"I'm not asking you to fall for anything. The fact that your wife was scuttled away before the bomb hit the White House isn't something that's up for debate. But I can lessen the impending consequences upon your return to Washington if you simply allow me to be a part of your administration, a virtual cabinet member, if you will. I need an answer now because I'm running out of time to help you."

"It's too late for that. You're going to attack Washington anyway—and not even you can stop those missiles."

Sinclair shrugged. "You can blame Al Fatihin— and I'll help you capture Evana Bahar. In fact, I'll help you capture a dozen of the most wanted terrorists in the world. What do you have to lose?"

Young sighed and looked at the ground. He didn't say a word as the seconds ticked past.

"I need an answer now," Sinclair said.

CHAPTER 29

HAWK AND ALEX HELD their ground for the next minute, fending off a growing number of guards. As Hawk scanned the area in between shots, he estimated there were now eight of Sinclair's men firing at his position from around the room. Hawk looked into his bag and realized he wasn't going to be able to withstand the assault much longer.

"Mia, are you still there?" he asked over the coms.

"Still here," she said. "Are you ready for me?"

"Almost. Can you tell where we are in the basement?"

"Yeah, I can see you on my screen."

"Okay," he said. "Can you disable the elevator and initiate a lockdown?"

"I'm still connected," she said. "All of the buildings functions were on a different system than the mainframe, so I've got access to the doors, gates, elevators, and security cameras in the facility."

"I'll give you the go-ahead when we're clear."

"Copy that," she said.

Hawk grabbed two smoke bombs out of his pack and opened the canisters before rolling them in the direction of the hostiles. When the smoke was sufficient to provide cover, he crouched low, shielding Alex as they hustled toward the elevator. Once they cross the threshold, they put their backs to the wall and pushed the button for the ground floor. Bullets peppered the elevator as the door closed, denting the aluminum. The moment they started to rise, he raised Mia on the coms.

"Commence the lockdown," he said.

"Got it," she said.

"I'll let you know once we're off the elevator so you can decommission it as well. That'll buy us enough time to get out of here."

Mia sighed, and Hawk immediately sensed something was wrong.

"What is it, Mia?" he asked.

"Well, I thought I should let you know that the coordinates I set for the missiles appear to have locked in," she said.

"That's great," Alex said. "Good work."

Mia groaned. "Uh, about that. You see, there's a slight problem."

"Spit it out, Mia," Hawk said.

"The coordinates I entered are for the facility."

"Which facility?" Hawk asked.

"The one you're in."

Hawk cursed as he looked at Alex and shook his head. "You do realize the President of the United States is in this building? Why wouldn't you just drop them harmlessly somewhere else, like the ocean?"

"I wasn't about to let this monster continue what he's doing," Mia said. "Besides, weren't you going to rescue the president anyway?"

"Well, he has his own Secret Service detail, so we figured he'd be fine once the threat was mitigated," Hawk said. "But I guess that's not the case anymore."

"Nor does President Young have any Secret Service members to help him," Mia said.

Hawk scowled. "What do you mean?"

"The security cameras show that all of the men who were with the president are knocked out in another room, their bodies piled on top of one another."

"Are they dead?" Alex asked.

"I'm not sure," Mia said. "I don't see any blood in the room. I'm just assuming they got knocked out by some kind of gas or injection."

Hawk sighed. "How many are there?"

"Four."

"Damn it," Hawk said. "How much time do we have?"

"At their current rate of speed, the missiles should strike the compound in just under ten minutes."

Hawk set his watch. "Roger that. Be ready to help the moment I ask for it—and we'll have a talk about this when we get back."

"I apologize for throwing a kink in your plan, but that would be a small sacrifice compared to what Sinclair plans to do to the world. And I think you would agree."

"We'll try to clean up your mess," Hawk said, "but I'm not happy about this. This is not how we operate."

Mia didn't say anything. Hawk muted his mic, and Alex followed suit.

"Can you believe this?" he asked.

"Don't blame me," she said, throwing her hands in the air.

"I'm not. I know this is what we get for bringing someone like her onboard. This would've been a much bigger disaster if we hadn't. But now, we don't have much time."

"We can still do this," she said.

"I hope you're right."

The elevator came to a stop, and outside was an eerie silence. Hawk nodded knowingly at Alex as she clutched the gun in her right hand, her left arm bloodied from the earlier encounter. He was worried that she wasn't up for the task.

"Are you okay?" he whispered.

"I'm great. Now let's get Young and get the hell off this island."

The doors slid open. Hawk and Alex didn't move.

After a pregnant pause, a hail of bullets poured inside.

CHAPTER 30

A MAN POKED HIS HEAD through the open door in Sinclair's control room. He glanced at his watch and then looked at Young, who still hadn't uttered a word. Sinclair marched over to his assistant to find out why he needed to be bothered yet again.

"This better be good," Sinclair said.

"Actually, I wish I had better news, but this is really urgent."

"Spit it out."

"Those missiles aren't headed to Washington, D.C., anymore."

Sinclair smiled. "Excellent. That'll give us time to figure things out. How is this possibly bad news?"

"They're headed straight for us."

"What?"

The man nodded. "We have less than eight minutes to evacuate the premises before impact."

Sinclair gritted his teeth and scanned the room. He'd planned for plenty of things, but this wasn't one of them. He needed to think, but there wasn't any time.

"Get everyone out of here," Sinclair said. "I'll handle this myself."

"But, sir, the American spy—"

"Where is he?"

"Last I heard they were still in the basement."

Sinclair nodded. "I'll lock the doors. Now run along and make sure nobody is left in the building."

"Should I make an announcement?"

"No. Call the department heads. Keep it quiet. If the American operative is still in the building, he'll be buried under the rubble with it, eliminating another problem for me."

"Yes, sir."

Sinclair closed the door and locked it so he wouldn't be bothered again.

"What's happening?" Karelin asked.

Sinclair ignored him. "I need a decision, President Young. Do you want to see your wife again? Do you want to save face, maybe even retain your position of power? If you do, say so right now, and I'll make it all happen."

Young took a deep breath and turned to face Sinclair. "I'm rejecting your offer. If my wife truly is alive and was involved in the White House explosion, she's betrayed both me and her country—and I don't want anything to do with her."

Sinclair clucked his tongue, shaking his head. "That's a shame, Mr. President. We could've been a great team. But next time I see you, if you're still alive, you'll probably be speaking Russian."

"Right now, I have some choice French words for you," Young said. "And I won't be begging for your pardon either when I say them."

Their conversation came to an abrupt end when the sound of gunshots echoed in the corridor just outside the room.

"Why is there shooting outside?" Karelin asked.

"It's nothing to concern yourself with," Sinclair said. "You're coming with me."

Young scowled. "You're just going to leave me here?"

Sinclair nodded. "I have no use for you anymore. How do you Americans say it, 'You've made your bed. Now lie in it'?"

The fighting outside the door grew louder and more furious.

CHAPTER 31

HAWK AND ALEX WAITED UNTIL the initial burst of bullets stopped. The door started to close when Hawk released his last smoke bomb, rolling it out into the hallway. The shooting restarted, forcing Hawk and Alex to stay hidden. Just as the two doors were about to meet, Hawk pressed the button, reopening them.

He stayed low, dashing to the right. Alex, who'd been on the opposite side of the elevator, followed after. They took cover behind what appeared to be a receptionist's desk.

"You still there, Mia?" Hawk asked after activating his microphone on his coms.

"What do you need?" she asked.

"Keep the elevator doors open, and I need you to tell me how to get to Young."

"You might need some help," she said. "There are four Secret Service men and four Russian security officers locked in a room a few meters down the hallway on your right. I saw a man lock up their weapons in a closet at the back."

"Roger that," Hawk said.

He crept down the corridor with Alex, and then they came to the room she'd directed them to. Once he opened the door, he found the men inside, just as she described. They were gagged and bound to chairs with ropes. Hawk explained the situation as he and Alex hustled around to each man, freeing them. Then Hawk repeated himself in Russian.

"We have seven minutes to retrieve our respective presidents and get out of here before a missile strikes this compound," Hawk said. "Does everyone understand?"

Heads bobbed, conveying that they realized the urgency of the situation.

Upon fetching all of their weapons, Hawk had the U.S. and Russian agents split up to attack the Obsidian guards. Meanwhile, he and Alex circumvented the main area, utilizing a back hallway that Mia had found to get them to Young unimpeded.

"Mia, we're almost there," Hawk said. "Are you ready?"

"Just give me the signal," she said.

They eased around the corner but jumped back when an unarmed man came hustling straight toward their position. Hawk pushed Alex back toward a doorway nook in the shadows and waited for the stranger to pass. Once he was gone, Hawk gestured to Alex to continue.

A few seconds later, they were standing outside the door.

"We're here," Hawk said.

"I'm opening the doors now," Mia said.

Fifteen seconds passed, and nothing happened.

Hawk checked his watch. Only five minutes remained before impact.

"What's going on? Why isn't anything happening?" he asked.

"I don't know," she said. "I'm doing the same thing I did every other time."

Alex pointed at the facial recognition box. "This entrance requires facial recognition. Do you think that could be it?"

"Maybe," Mia said. "I don't know. I just know that whatever I was doing before isn't working now."

Hawk stepped back and surveyed the area. The opaque glass prevented him from seeing whatever was taking place inside. He could make out at least two silhouetted figures moving around the room, but nothing more.

"Think this glass is bulletproof?" Hawk asked.

Alex shrugged. "There's only way to find out."

He stepped back and fired a shot at the glass. It

spidered, and then he kicked at it with his foot. As he did, a bullet came from inside the room.

Hawk jumped back, avoiding getting hit. Almost all the glass burst out and spread across the floor. He peered around the edge and saw Sinclair wielding a gun.

"Hold tight," Hawk said, easing back and then looking at Alex. "Sinclair's armed."

Hawk trained his weapon in front of him and moved around the now open door. He locked eyes with Sinclair as he jammed the nozzle of his pistol into Young's head.

"That's far enough," Sinclair said. "You make another move, and I'm going to put a bullet in your president's head."

Hawk didn't flinch. "You'll do no such thing. If I see your trigger finger even twitch, you'll be dead before you can fire. This is the end of the line, Sinclair."

"You must be the infamous Brady Hawk," Sinclair said.

Hawk wasn't in the mood for flattery and didn't budge.

"I managed to co-opt your boss, but I underestimated you," Sinclair said. "I should've had my men deal more severely with you when you first appeared on our radar."

"We all have regrets," Hawk said, refusing to inquire about Sinclair's revelation regarding Blunt. "Now, just send President Young over to me unless you want to die."

Perspiration streamed down Young's face, his eyes full of fear. A few feet to Sinclair's right stood the Russian president, whose hands were raised in a gesture of surrender.

"I don't want to hurt anybody," Sinclair said. "But I will if you don't back away."

"You're not the one calling the shots here, *mate*," Hawk said with a sneer. "You back away from the president and drop your weapon before I put a hole in your head."

Sinclair tightened his grip on Young, eliciting a moan from the president. "I don't think you're fast enough, so here's how this is going to go down. I'm backing out this door with President Karelin, and when I'm gone, you can have your gutless president. But don't try to come after me. You'll regret it."

Alarms sounded in the building, whooping a warning. A robotic woman's voice made an announcement. "Everyone, please exit the building immediately. You have one minute to evacuate the premises."

Sinclair edged toward the door, still holding Young. Hawk wanted to take a shot, but he realized the risk was too great. The Australian billionaire wasn't to be reasoned with and appeared mentally unstable given the stakes of the situation.

Sinclair edged backward, taking baby steps as he went. When he reached the door on the far side of the room, he forced it open with his back, urging Karelin to go first. Once they were both almost inside, Sinclair shoved Young forward. He stumbled and then slid headfirst along the floor. The door clicked behind Sinclair as he peered through the small glass slit before darting off.

Hawk and Alex hustled over to help Young to his feet.

"Are you all right, Mr. President?" Hawk asked.

"I'm better now," Young said.

Hawk ushered Young toward the door. "Well, we need to get out of here right now."

"Hawk! Alex!" Mia's voice crackled on the coms. "You don't have a second to lose."

Hawk hustled toward the door, talking as he went. "What do you mean?"

"Sinclair just initiated a self-destruct sequence," Mia said. "You have ninety seconds to get out of that building before it implodes. It's going to hit before the missiles get there."

"We've gotta go now," Hawk said, gesturing for the president to move.

They hustled down the hallway and then came to a stop when they heard gunfire from around the corner.

"What are you doing, Hawk?" Alex asked. "We can't contemplate this. We need to run now or we're not going to make it."

Hawk wasn't afraid of the shooting. His eyes were locked in on an abandoned cart in the hallway.

"Get on, Mr. President," Hawk said, nodding toward the makeshift vehicle. "If we're going to make it out alive, I'm gonna have to help you."

Young hoisted one of his legs on the top shelf of the cart, while Hawk and Alex steadied the wheels. When the president was stabilized, Hawk started pushing. As he rounded the corner, he saw two guards firing at Secret Service members. He nodded at Alex and mouthed for her to take the guy on the right.

They fired two shots each, felling the Obsidian agents. "Don't shoot," Hawk cried. "They're both dead."

As they rounded the corner, the Secret Service agents holstered their weapons and rushed over to President Young.

Hawk waved them away. "We don't have time for this. The building is about to explode. Run for the exits, and don't look back."

All the men complied but one, who joined Hawk

in pushing Young down the hallway. When they reached the doors, Hawk helped Young, carrying him with the assistance of the other agent. They hustled down the steps and rushed outside.

Hawk had a clock ticking in his head.

Five . . . four . . . three . . .

His feet were moving as fast as he could as he scanned the area for some sort of cover from the explosion. He eyed the guardhouse near the edge of the fence as a place to protect them from the blast. Steering Young toward the structure, they all fell in line. Hawk shielded Alex, while the other agents gathered around Young.

Two . . . one . . .

CHAPTER 32

Washington, D.C.

THE WIND WHISTLED PAST Titus Black as he descended toward the ground in a free fall. A HALO jump was deemed the best way to approach the outpost where J.D. Blunt's niece, Morgan, was being held by Sinclair's henchmen. While Blunt was away in Europe, tending to Hawk's and Alex's issues, Blunt received a report from one of his contacts at the NSA detailing the exact location of Blunt's niece.

When Black's feet hit the ground, he rolled, spreading out the impact from his fall. He gathered up his parachute and hid it beneath a rock. It was only 4:00 a.m. in New Mexico, a half-hour drive from the entrance to Carlsbad Cavern National Park—and 6:00 a.m. in Washington, where J.D. Blunt was wide awake and watching the whole operation from the Phoenix Foundation headquarters via Black's body camera.

Black made his way along a dirt road, one utilized

only by ranchers and recreational thrill seekers who liked to roar across vast stretches of unpopulated land on their motorcycles. But at this time of morning, the only things roaming around were rats and rattlesnakes.

On a distant hill, Black saw the silhouette of the small clapboard house. Not a single light shone, which wasn't shocking. He was certain electricity wasn't available in such a remote place.

As he approached the house, he didn't notice any guards outside. He circled the structure twice before deciding to go inside. The wooden steps creaked as he approached as stealthily as possible. However, the sounds must've been loud enough to wake Morgan's hostage taker.

The *thump, thump, thump* from inside the house vibrated the porch where Black was standing. He trained his gun in front of him and prepared for it to swing open. Seconds later when it did, Black smashed the man's hand, sending his gun flying.

Black put two bullets in the man before rushing inside. He found Morgan curled up in a fetal position, her tear-stained cheeks glistening beneath the glow of his flashlight.

"It's all right," Black said. "You're safe now. Your uncle sent me. In fact, he's watching right now."

Morgan embraced Black and began sobbing. He dug some clothes out of his pack and gave them to her along with some privacy to change. While she was putting on more appropriate attire for the cool temperatures outside, Black called Blunt.

"If you were watching, you know I've got her," Black said.

"I know," Blunt said, his voice quivering. "I didn't know if I'd ever see her again."

"You will soon enough. Just let the pilot know that he needs to get the plane gassed up and ready to go. We'll be ready to leave in half an hour."

"You got it, champ," Blunt said before he hung up.

When Morgan was finished, Black led her outside, warning her to watch her step as the hostile's body lay lifeless on the porch. He stepped over the corpse and held his hand out to help her. She froze and then spit on him before stomping on his head.

"Take that," she said before calling him a whole slew of names as she repeatedly kicked him.

Black grabbed her and bear-hugged her, pulling her away from the body. "It's okay now. He's gone, and you're safe."

She broke down again and started crying. Black carried her over to the man's Jeep and placed her in the passenger seat before hustling around to the driver's side. He ignited the engine with the twist of the key and roared off toward the airport.

* * *

A HALF HOUR LATER, Blunt hung up with Black, who reported that they'd safely arrived at the airport and were preparing for takeoff. For the first time in over two weeks, Blunt felt like he could breathe. He clipped off the end of a cigar and jammed it into his mouth. While too early to drink a celebratory toast, he wouldn't wait long before popping open one of his favorite bourbon bottles.

He thanked Shields for her help during the mission and returned to his office. On his desk, he found a piping hot cup of coffee and the morning's paper. He had just settled in to read about the upcoming G8 summit when his phone rang.

"This is Blunt," he said as he answered.

"Well, Mr. Blunt," said Falcon Sinclair, "I wanted to let you know that I've decided not to keep my end of the bargain since you broke yours."

"I broke our bargain? What are you talking about?"

"I told you if you tried to dissuade the president from coming with me that your niece would be killed."

"And I never breathed a word to him about it," Blunt said. "All I did was encourage him to go."

"As well as send a team after him."

"You think I'm just going to let you take President

Young on some joy ride and not at least have an eye on him? Think again."

"No matter," Sinclair said. "It's your niece who will pay the price. She's such a sweet young woman. I hate to have to needlessly take her life, but there are consequences. And what kind of man would I be if I didn't keep my word?"

"Well, seeing that your kidnapper couldn't keep Morgan and is dead in the New Mexico desert, I doubt you can keep your word in this case. But I promise, I won't hold it against you."

"You're gonna pay for this."

"No," Blunt said, "I'm gonna have my men hunt you down and kill you like they did Osama bin Laden or Saddam Hussein. Better watch your back."

Blunt hung up and smiled. He couldn't wait to hear from Hawk and find out how they'd managed to rattle Sinclair so much.

CHAPTER 33

Rutland Island, Indian Ocean

HAWK WATCHED THE OBSIDIAN facility implode, turning the entire building into a raging inferno. He urged everyone to their feet and directed them farther away from the perimeter. They ran, refusing to stop until they found a spot behind a small hill. Alex grabbed his hand as a pair of missiles rained down on the compound, turning what was left of it into little more than ash.

"I thought we weren't gonna make it," she said in a hushed tone to Hawk.

"When we're together, I never count us out, even when the odds are stacked against us," he said.

President Young turned to Hawk. "Thank you for coming after me. If you hadn't, I don't know—"

The president stopped, unable to find the words. A tear streaked down his face.

"It's all right to cry, Mr. President," Alex said.

"That was terribly traumatic."

"I'm not crying about what happened today," Young said. "I'm crying about Madeline."

Hawk helped Young stand, and they started down the road back toward the tent in silence. Alex finally put her arm around him.

"It's always tough when we lose someone," she said.

"That's the thing," Young said. "I didn't really lose her. She left."

Hawk drew back, eying Young carefully. "What do you mean?"

Does he know?

"According to Falcon Sinclair, Madeline helped set up the bombing on the White House," Young said. "Apparently, she's living it up by a pool somewhere in some tropical paradise. And I've been played for a fool."

"Do you want us to track her down?" Hawk asked.

"No, I don't think that's a good idea. If she wanted out of our marriage, she didn't need to be a traitor to do it. I just wish she would've at least talked to me about it."

"So, what next?" Hawk asked. "I will relish the opportunity to go after Falcon Sinclair. And it'll be our pleasure to deliver his dead body to you."

Young sighed. "As much as I'd like that right now, we must remain singular in our focus and capture Evana Bahar."

"But the truth is that she wasn't even responsible for the bombing at the White House," Alex said.

"That doesn't matter. Perception is reality in today's world. And if you listen to all the pundits and commentators out there, I'm weak on national security. I need a win there something fierce. You two think you can deliver that for me?"

Hawk nodded and glanced at Alex. "She certainly deserves to be held accountable for her crimes against our country."

"Good," Young said. "I'll consider it done. And once you finish with her, I want you to raze Falcon Sinclair's entire empire."

"Of course, Mr. President," Hawk said. "It'll be my honor to finish that job for you."

When they returned to the tent, they contacted the president's team in Kuala Lumpur to discreetly alert them to what had happened while they were gone. A helicopter was ordered to retrieve the president. The pilot notified Hawk that he'd return shortly to pick up everyone else along with their equipment.

After the chopper disappeared on the horizon, Hawk turned to Mia. "We need to talk."

"Look, I know what you're going to say," she said. "And I'm sorry. The president seems like a good man who cares about his people. I let my rage take over—and I know it put many lives at risk."

"Not just many lives—the life of the President of the United States," Hawk said.

"I know, I know. I promise it'll never happen again."

Hawk cocked his head to one side. "Again? What makes you think you'll be asked to assist us in the future?"

"Please, won't you?" Mia asked, clasping her hands together as if she were about to offer a prayer "This venture has made me realize that I need to put my talent to work for something worthwhile, something that actually helps keep people safe, not just ruins the lives of others who I deem to be evil."

"I'm not sure we can trust you," Alex said.

"You can," Mia shot back emphatically. "I won't let you down again. I swear."

"Well, we're not the decision makers when it comes to who partners with us on our missions, but I might put in a kind word for you if you're serious," Hawk said.

"Yes, please do," Mia said. "This was one incredible operation. If it's like this all the time, I can't wait to join your team."

Hawk shrugged. "We'll see what the boss has to say about it. In the meantime, let's get everything together. I can't wait to get off this island."

* * *

HAWK ENTERED THE Phoenix Foundation headquarters three days later with Alex. They convened in the conference room to discuss the recent mission. Blunt was already gnawing on a cigar when he started the discussion.

"We're all here," Blunt said. "And at this point, that might be the most important thing."

"Being alive is good," Alex said.

"But we're not done yet," Hawk said. "Not by a long shot."

"No, we're not," Blunt said. "But I just received a bit of intel this morning regarding Al Fatihin's next big strike."

"I know that's not what you want to do right now," Hawk said.

Blunt shook his head. "No, it's not. I want to put Sinclair in a vice and grind him until he shatters into a million pieces. But that'll have to wait. We need to get a win for the president. And then we're going to obliterate Falcon Sinclair and Obsidian."

THE END

ABOUT THE AUTHOR

R.J. PATTERSON is an award-winning writer living in southeastern Idaho. He first began his illustrious writing career as a sports journalist, recording his exploits on the soccer fields in England as a young boy. Then when his father told him that people would pay him to watch sports if he would write about what he saw, he went all in. He landed his first writing job at age 15 as a sports writer for a daily newspaper in Orangeburg, S.C. He later attended earned a degree in newspaper journalism from the University of Georgia, where he took a job covering high school sports for the award-winning *Athens Banner-Herald* and *Daily News*.

He later became the sports editor of *The Valdosta Daily Times* before working in the magazine world as an editor and freelance journalist. He has won numerous writing awards, including a national award for his investigative reporting on a sordid tale surrounding an NCAA investigation over the University of Georgia football program.

R.J. enjoys the great outdoors of the Northwest while living there with his wife and four children. He still follows sports closely. He also loves connecting with readers and would love to hear from you. To stay updated about future projects, connect with him over Facebook or on the interwebs at www.RJPbooks.com and sign up for his newsletter.

Made in the USA
Coppell, TX
04 August 2022